D0378934

ALSO BY DJUNA

Everything Good Dies Here
(translated by Adrian Thieret)

COUNTERWEIGHT

COUNTERWEIGHT

DJUNA

Translated from the Korean
by Anton Hur

Pantheon Books
New York

This book is published with the support of the Literature Translation Institute of Korea (LTI Korea).

Pantheon Books and colophon are registered trademarks of Penguin Random House LLC.

Library of Congress Cataloging-in-Publication Data
Names: Djuna [Tyuna], author. Hur, Anton, translator.
Title: Counterweight : a novel / Djuna ; translated from the Korean by Anton Hur.
Other titles: P'yŏnghyŏngch'u. English
Description: First American edition. New York : Pantheon Books, 2023
Identifiers: LCCN 2022053643 (print). LCCN 2022053644 (ebook).
ISBN 9780593317211 (hardcover). ISBN 9780593317228 (ebook).
Subjects: LCGFT: Science fiction. Novels.
Classification: LCC PL994.235 P9613 2022 (print) |
LCC PL994.235 (ebook) | DDC 895.73/5—dc23/eng/20221221
LC record available at https://lccn.loc.gov/2022053643
LC ebook record available at https://lccn.loc.gov/2022053644

www.pantheonbooks.com

Jacket design and illustration by Tal Goretsky

Printed in the United States of America
First American Edition
2 4 6 8 9 7 5 3 1

If I have to climb to heaven on a ladder,
I shall decline the invitation.

—MERCEDES McCAMBRIDGE

HOUSE OF HAN

Han Bugyeom
(former president of LK Group)

Jung Somi ------- Han Junghyuk (adopted)
(former president of LK Group)

Han Sahyun ------- Kim Lena

Han Suhyun
(current CEO of LK Space)
(biological son of Han Bugyeom)

Kim Jaein ------ Anton Choi
(head of LK Space Development Research Center)
(biological child of Kim Lena)

PROLOGUE

Santa Teresa, California

"Your mother is going to be a star," said the man in the gray uniform.

The child stared at the wooden box the man was handing her. Inside was a blue glass jar containing her mother's white ashes. The girl pulled her left hand from her trouser pocket and stroked the bottle with the tip of her index finger until her hand accidentally brushed against the man's, making him jump as if he'd been shocked by electricity. The girl took a step back.

"That's not my mom."

Puzzled, the man checked the label of the jar. It was the girl's mother, all right. But who knows. Every family has a story. Perhaps the woman who'd brought her in just now was her "real" mother.

Reading the man's expression, the girl quickly shook her head.

"That's not my mom. It's just ashes."

Ah, a little philosopher. He supposed the girl was right. It *was* just ashes, the powdery remains of a few earthly elements.

What did it mean to have briefly been a human body in the long history of these elements that began some hundreds of millions of years ago inside a supernova? They'll be mixed into some fireworks and fired up into the air, turning the sky rose-colored for a moment before scattering in the wind and going on their way.

The child's other mother walked in, a slender woman and a striking beauty. Did she say she was an actress? Well, someone famous, but the man had a hard time telling Asian women apart. She spoke to the man in an accent that was hard to place and signed the tablet. Its lid now firmly shut, the box was moved to the next room, where its contents were to be mixed into gunpowder.

That night, when the fireworks started from the yacht, the dead mother's ghost was sitting to the left of the child. The mother's speech and gesture data, accumulated by the secretary program's avatar, made the augmented-reality ghost look alive and real. The child thought about her mother's ashes brightening up and spreading out in the sky, and also about the ghost sitting next to her. She imagined the information that had once constituted the mind of an individual scattering and fading into the night.

The fireworks were her mother. Not because they contained the powder that for a moment had made up her mother, but because the yacht, the funeral, and the fireworks were all planned by her. What the child was seeing was an extension of her mother's thoughts and wishes.

It's just that no one had expected to see it so soon.

COUNTERWEIGHT

HUMMINGBIRD ATTACK

Clink. Clink. Clink. A nickel and a quarter are dancing on Rex Tamaki's left hand.

Controlled by tiny movements of the index and little fingers, these thin metal discs fly up, spin, roll, and leapfrog over each other like they're living beings with free will.

The dance of the coins ends as abruptly as it started. Realizing he was distracting me, Tamaki snatches the coins from the air and drops them into his pocket, throwing me a smirk. A provocative and seductive smirk. Tamaki isn't gay, he just enjoys pushing buttons and stringing people along. Miffed, I look away.

The interior of the plane is quiet. The only thing I hear through my nonaugmented ears is the low drone of the engines. This apparent silence is deceptive; judging from the continuous smirking of Tamaki's personnel, I can tell they're sending silent messages to each other. They did open a channel for me, too, but since I entered the cabin not one person has engaged me in conversation. Not that I care. They can keep their stupid jokes.

Rex Tamaki, contrasting with his gorilla-like colleagues

with their muscles bursting out of their shirts, looks almost slight. But you can't trust looks these days. No one's strength is in proportion to their muscles anymore. Since he lost his Olympic gold medal fifteen years ago in a doping scandal, Tamaki's body has undergone several phases of modification. The current version, now before me, is clearly the handiwork of someone who treats rules and regulations with contempt.

The alarm inside my head strikes 22:00. For the next eighteen hours, judicial power of the Gondal Quarter will transfer from Tamoé's government to the LK Group. Don't even ask me what I had to do flitting between islands, trying to make this happen.

Tamaki and his gang, almost synchronized, get up from their seats. I feel a kind of floating sensation as we begin to descend and the golden hatch in front of me spins open. Our Hummingbird circles over the Gondal Quarter at three hundred meters and descends like an elevator. Through the widening hatch, I can see the coastline village that looks like a scattering of plastic boxes.

As the hatch widens and the plane begins to slow down at fifteen meters, the Tamaki gang begin jumping off one by one. Despite their bulky bodies they move with such grace that their feet hardly make a sound as they land on the roofs of the buildings and disappear into the village. I remain secured in my seat, seatbelt fastened, looking on.

Hot air blows through the hatch into the interior. It smells of the village. Food, fish, excrement, trash, people.

In that mess of boxes are thousands of people breathing, eating, excreting, sleeping, vomiting, copulating, and popping out babies. My insides turn.

"Shall we have some fun, Mac?"

Tamaki's voice. And like all voices that come over the Worm, it's oddly separated from ambient noise. The voice of a god, stripped of its sanctity, with only the monstrosity remaining.

An augmented-reality screen blinks on before me. Red and blue dots stud the village. The blue dots are LK's Security operatives, the red dots are Patusans of the Liberation Front, who one month earlier had assassinated three Doran Party figures in Pala. I turn to a second window, where I have a POV of the blue dots. White foam is flung in the face of a red dot who holds up an AK-1 at the face of a blue dot. Another red dot throws a fist at a blue dot and is flung backward by one retaliatory kick. A third red dot has already bitten down on a gun and fired off half his face. A blue dot is ripping children off his body, ragamuffins who have flung themselves on him like a school of sharks.

I go back to the first window. Now there isn't a single red dot on its own. They're all surrounded by blue dots and, as of a few seconds ago, are moving toward a yellow dot in the village. The current time is 11:13. Tamaki had predicted the operation would be over in fifteen minutes.

Our Hummingbird, its hatch still open, moves toward the yellow dot. A small plaza in the village, just big enough for the Hummingbird to land and for people to move around the plane.

When I disembark, I ignore the men under restraint whose faces are messy with foam and who are being dragged onto the plane. I walk toward where the last red dot is at a standstill at a northern building. The children who had only a moment ago swarmed the security force agents, screaming and biting, are gazing at us expressionlessly.

The door of the house of the red dot is half open. As a colleague stands next to him, transmitting the video of the scene, Tamaki hammers a short pipe into the dead man's skull.

"And what do you hope to gain from that?" I ask.

"The dead remember a surprising number of things."

I leave him to his harvest of memories and consider the rest of the information coming through the Worm, the data inside the captured terrorists' memory devices being gathered and categorized. I scratch my head, irritated. Never will my body understand how this many things can be happening while there's nothing for my hands to do.

The information I'm looking for is mostly about internal spies, moles. We don't care about the assassination incident itself that prompted our intervention. As with most Doran Party members, dead people are largely irrelevant, more useful dead than alive. Though LK verified the identities and locations of two of the assassins within a couple of days of the incident, we never shared that information with the Pala government, and for good reason.

The list of 154 people, names obtained from today's operation and sorted by Security HQ computers, comes up on the screen.

Of these, only about thirty are of any consequence, and LK's External Affairs, which is my division, are interested in nine. Seven of these are midgrade officers at LK, two are Patusan municipal workers. They will all be put on a watch list and neglected. The information we've obtained today has the shelf life of a mere two weeks, not enough time to waste on arrests or disclosures.

I add the summarized information to the report for External Affairs and look over the remaining names and faces on the list. Mostly people who were relatives of those arrested today or various personnel they had designated as their targets. A few of them might have actual ties with the Liberation Front, but for most it's just a matter of being accounted for.

The scrolling list pauses. A new window opens with information and photographs. Boring haircut, fairly handsome man in his late twenties. Name: Choi Gangwu. An LK Space worker, and the only Korean on the list. Why did I save this man's information? It bothers me for a moment that I can't remember.

Oh right. Now I do. That Korean guy who wouldn't laser off his beard.

A SOMEWHAT SUSPICIOUS
NEW GUY AT WORK

The first time I saw Choi Gangwu was in a cafeteria, seventeen levels underground, in Patusan. Ross Lee had insisted on having the 232nd anniversary of LK Group's founding there, which meant everyone was incredibly busy. Managing to extricate myself with great difficulty, I fled downstairs, where neither Ross Lee nor Han Suhyun could find me. The city's waterfall of escalators eventually led me to the employee cafeteria.

It was crawling with newly hired techies flown in from Seoul and Jeonju. Everyone wore similar clothes regardless of gender, and all had the same neat business face. Every unit had a table and was eating from the same menu, and I got the impression that even their chopsticks and spoons were moving to a kind of rhythm. They seemed a little cowed by their new surroundings, or even scared.

I spotted Choi Gangwu because of his five-o'clock shadow. He was the only Korean man in that cafeteria who had not lasered off his facial hair. It struck me as a bit of pitiful personal rebellion. Why insist on shaving every day when you're not even allowed to grow a beard? Look at me, I'm so very special among my identical peers.

Once I noticed his face, other aspects of his appearance

came to my attention. Like I said before, he was "fairly" handsome. But not as neatly so as the people sitting by him. His face wasn't exactly symmetrical, he had rough skin, and his big eyes and mouth gave him a famished look.

Not the kind of face LK likes. No chance he'd work in customer service.

Curious, I scanned his face and looked through his personnel files. They weren't much to speak of. He'd gone to mediocre schools and received mediocre grades. Getting into LK on his third attempt, he surprisingly managed to rank second highest on the entrance exam.

The company must've been suspicious of this, since they challenged him with a difficult interview, but he passed that as well. It did make me wonder how he did it, but not enough to actually find out.

I stored his information on the Worm and forgot about it.

And here we were, eight months later, his name popping out of a memory device owned by Patusan Liberation Front assassins.

Back on the Hummingbird, I sit down in my seat, put my seatbelt on tight, and contemplate the information about Choi Gangwu sent over the Worm. Most of it was put together by someone from the Liberation Front referred to with the initials ZS, who was apparently trying to poach LK employees. The files were haphazard and poorly organized.

According to the report, ZS had met Choi Gangwu around the mouth of the Jewel River two months ago. Choi Gangwu had waded into the mud to take a photograph of an emerald butterfly sitting on a discarded Coke can and gotten stuck. ZS helped pull him out of the mud and they ended up having dinner together. The next day Choi Gangwu landed on the target list. The motive? According to the very logical reasoning of the report, Choi Gangwu liked butterflies, which meant he was an environmentalist, and all environmentalists were anti-corporates. The fact that environmentalists were actually supportive of the Patusan space elevator construction project or that Choi Gangwu had desperately tried to be hired by LK for three whole years was duly ignored. That kind of fine detail was for management to pore over. It was more important for ZS to have a Korean permanent-contract worker on his list.

ZS kept in contact with Choi Gangwu. They dropped in on his quarters and introduced him to the butterfly collectors and environmental activists of Patusan. No need to mention that some of them were Liberation Front members.

The seduction effort went on for about a month before fizzling out.

It seems that despite their hopes of luring a permanent-contract worker to their side, Choi Gangwu wasn't the ideal target. He was a model LK employee, and whenever there was even the slightest whiff of controversy, he would make his excuses and leave. According to the final report, the Liberation Front was disappointed not only by this behavior but also by his low position within the company, which was only a step above intern. Of course they had thought he ranked higher than he did. He was five years older than his corporate cohort, and looked it, too.

So now what? We can use Choi Gangwu and ZS's relationship to infiltrate the Liberation Front. But what would be the point of that? We have enough info to identify ZS and easily go up their chain of command to smoke them out without involving Choi Gangwu. Getting some untrained office worker to do the work of real spies is the kind of thing you'll only see in novels.

I decide to leave Choi Gangwu alone. This is all just extrane-
ous info. No reason for it to leave External Affairs. If it continues to bother me, I'll just bring him in for an interrogation. But
there's no reason to make his already thorny path through the
corporate wilds even worse.

PATUSAN

A cross-shaped island country at the end of the Brierly archi-
pelago. A respectably thick tropical forest with pitifully low
biodiversity, a uselessly high extinct volcano in the middle of
the island, and villages and cities that had collapsed after drain-
ing their aquifers with no consideration of the consequences.
And, of course, some truly beautiful butterflies.

Before LK subsumed it, that was the kind of place Patusan
was.

Fifteen years ago, when LK announced that they would build
the space elevator on Patusan, the people's first reaction was
to wonder why they'd do such a foolish thing. LK was already
using skyhooks to send three or four spaceships a year beyond
Earth's atmosphere. Enough for people to believe that the true
Age of Space was finally upon us.

Skyhooks were relatively easier to make, and were light, fun,
and fast. Compared to them, the large and slow space elevators
seemed as archaic as blimps. Beautiful and grand, but completely unnecessary.

What people didn't know was that while LK continued to
develop their skyhooks, they were little by little building up

the technological infrastructure for space elevators. The space elevator was no longer merely a dream proposed by speculative fiction writers of old.

It became a thing that was both feasible and profitable in the real world.

And what better place to realize this plan than a run-down island nation where two-thirds of the population had already immigrated to the two neighboring island nations, Pala and Tamoé?

Patusan is to become a gateway to Earth.

A satellite in geosynchronous orbit dropped a spider cable that began automated work on the elevator long before it touched land. Once it did make landfall, the cable grew thicker and wider and longer and more complex. The factory on the island is still busy constructing this pathway to space, and the work will not stop as long as the company remains solvent.

Around that site, the Patusan economy is beginning to revive. Once down to four thousand residents, the island's population now reaches eighty-nine thousand. There's a new harbor, airport, and city connecting them to the summit of the mountain where the elevator touches down. People from all over the world have moved there to help with the effort of paving a way into space.

Not everyone is happy about it. Patusan now belongs to a transnational corporation. Its government is an empty shell.

No matter how much money LK pours into the country, the Indigenous people are not satisfied. They've mostly been relegated to the margins, unable to find a place in the new city's systems. The people who had fled to Pala and Tamoé weren't even given their share of compensation. From somewhere between these three islands, the Patusan Liberation Front is born. Bombs explode, people die. Their pockets are unexpectedly deep, their money never runs out; sponsors have jumped into the fray, keen to use them to make a buck.

And it's my job to deal with them.

I turn my gaze to the screen on the desk before me. From each of its three windows, a different face looks back at me. The slender one in the center is Ross Lee, current president of the LK Group. Only twenty years ago he was the most creative engineer on the planet. Our ability to mass-produce LK tubes, the building blocks of the elevator, is thanks to this man's genius. But now he's just a scarecrow, hired to avoid anti-chaebol prosecution. He would rather be at the opera or ballet at this hour, but here he is instead, receiving a report on some incident he doesn't care about. The thin-lipped man next to him is Han Suhyun, CEO of LK Space, who is also the son of the late Han Junghyuk, former president of LK. He thinks he's already the de facto head of the LK Group, but there's still a long way to go. The woman on the right is Nia Abbas, the city's mayor and second in terms of political clout to the Prime Minister of Patusan. But considering how the Patusan government is being funded by LK, one does wonder about the point of having titles at all.

"The assassin suspects were arrested two hours ago in Pala," I say. "We did not provide the authorities with information from our side. Either the Pala police were more competent than we thought or the Indonesian government has intervened. It could've been the Indonesian government that funded the Gondal Quarter gang. I can verify this within two days.

"All the people on the list obtained from this operation are now being surveilled by the police. Interrogation is meaningless. The individuals seem to know very little. A few think they know more than they actually do, but the organization isn't as fragile as that. We've got to see all the parts moving together before we can determine what's controlling the Front from above.

"The important thing isn't how the authorities are interpreting what went down in the Gondal Quarter. It's the fact that we can still get additional information no matter which side is the one that finds it."

"Was that really necessary?" says Ross Lee. "Couldn't we have requested information and cooperation from Pala and Tamoé?"

"The blood had to stain someone's hands. Better LK's than anyone else's. We followed all legal processes. We stopped fanatics who have the potential to wage terrorism on a global scale. It's impossible to do that without hurting anyone. Someone had to die. LK, in this inevitable situation, just happens to have a tiny bit to gain. Can we really call that selfish? When the elevator tower is the most important asset humanity possesses?"

Han Suhyun smiles faintly and nods. He's feeling his power coursing through his veins, thanks to the murderous activities in the Gondal Quarter. The operation wouldn't have been possible without him signing off on it. The more uncomfortable Ross Lee feels over the killings perpetrated by LK, the better Han Suhyun's position becomes.

As the mayor starts nitpicking over the report put together by External Affairs, the talk turns tedious. I mechanically recite the prepared answers and get ready to leave the meeting. Though I do need to squeeze in some impressive last words before I part. Something to keep Ross Lee and Han Suhyun from looking down their noses at me.

A notification window appears on the left. I'm thrown off by its first sentence: "New entry detected. H & H Warehouse, Bandar Seri Begawan. By renter Damon Chu."

A MAN OF FAINT EXISTENCE

Damon Chu has been working at LK Space's External Affairs for seven years. An American with a Korean mother and a Chinese father. Thirty-five and single. Fourth year working in the city of Bandar Seri Begawan.

The tiny problem here is that Damon Chu doesn't actually exist.

And there's no irony in that statement.

Whether an actual Damon Chu exists has never mattered. Either way, this man has been one of the LK Group's countless work-from-home employees, going about their days as usual. Sometimes, he's even more useful than his living colleagues. He has no opinions, will, or desires. You can send him anywhere, fire him at any time. If the political situation gets too tricky, you can even kill him. I don't know how other people feel, but in my book, not having to kill an actual person when someone needs to die is a pretty big plus. LK Space alone has about seventeen of these mannequins and I'm sure there are even more throughout the conglomerate.

Damon Chu was invented by me and the former president Han Junghyuk. I like to think of him as our son. In fact, I mixed in about 30 percent of President Han's and my appearances when creating him. Fifty-fifty seemed a little gross. We created him as a disposable fix for a certain legal problem, and once the problem was solved, left him to circulate in the veins of the LK Group. Damon Chu had by now accumulated fifteen thousand International Credits, a little real estate, and an H & H storage locker—a fairly impressive worker. The former president was now dead and only I knew Chu's true identity, which meant his assets were mine. I thought of him as an inheritance from the late president. Although I'm too busy to spend my own pay at the moment, it's nice to know I'm twenty-one thousand credits in the black.

Until this nonexistent meddler showed up at H & H, trying to steal what's mine. New entry detected? Really?

Undaunted, I call H & H. Though unfortunately all I have access to is the information on the screen. Not long ago I would've been able to ask a friend from the Bandar Seri Begawan police for help, but that's no longer possible, now that administration has been handed over to AI. What other tricks can I use? I think for a moment before looking up our list of employees in that city. Not that I think any one of them is pretending to be Damon Chu. But just as a starting point.

Five employees seem to have gone on vacation together. One of them is Choi Gangwu.

I look up his hotel.

It's not five hundred meters away from H & H. I send a message to his phone and track his location. Choi Gangwu is one hundred meters away from the warehouse and walking toward the hotel. He has taken something that is small enough to put in his pocket or a bag.

What could it be? Not the Tintin poster signed by Hergé. That's a relief. Because it really is something I could never bear to part with. What else is in there? A little cash, some expensive furniture, an Aramaic scroll of dubious provenance I bought during the Vatican's going-out-of-business sale, lurid artworks the president had not wanted to pass on to any of his progeny, some evidence I can't get rid of concerning illegal activity that won't hurt anyone as long as no one knows about it for the next eleven years. That storage locker is also my ammunition depot. Not that I would have any occasion to go all the way to Bandar Seri Begawan to wave my guns around.

How does Choi Gangwu have information on Damon Chu? The information leak is unfortunate but possible. There's no such thing as perfect secrecy in this world. But why Damon Chu? This scarecrow's secret is so deeply buried as to be useless. If the Indonesian police ever find the locker it'll be annoying, but all I'll have to do is blame some dead person. The other thing is that whoever has the power to reveal Damon Chu's identity would never make such an awkward mistake and get exposed like this.

I pore over Choi Gangwu's information one more time. His parents have both passed. His mother died seventeen years ago, when North American white supremacists spread the Crusader virus in Asia and Africa, and his father died in a hiking accident nine years later.

His only living family is a sister, two years older. She almost died four years ago from the Azikiwe disease. Her treatment had been covered by insurance, but full recovery takes a lot more money than that. Ah, and Choi Gangwu's father had some kind of conflict with LK. A common enough situation, where a private inventor should've hired an agent before letting a conglomerate steal their idea. His invention had been for one of the thousands of components that provide power for the spiders crawling up into the Patusan sky. The police did suspect foul play, but not strongly enough to investigate further.

A man who joins LK to avenge his father. A trope from old Korean dramas. But this level of information would've been known to HR. There was also the additional interview, the psych test and polygraph, and an investigation into how his scores had jumped so high. The company had known everything I knew—no, more than I knew—but still took him on as an employee.

Is it the company and not the Liberation Front that's planning a conspiracy?

What if all these suspicious bits of private information are just bait? Part of a trap the company had laid for the Liberation Front? But that's impossible. There's no way such an undertaking would've been done without me. But what if?

A conspiracy that doesn't involve me? Am I now as disposable as Damon Chu? What do I have that that scarecrow doesn't have, anyway? Criminal records in three countries, no family or friends, stateless. My only safety net, which was President Han, died two years ago, and there are plenty of others to take my place. It's perfectly plausible that there's someone in the company who considers me a leftover from President Han's regime and wants me removed.

After some hesitation, I leave my apartment. I glance up at Patusan City, which looks like a waterfall of light flowing down from the mountain. Choi Gangwu's apartment is 150 meters up and 700 meters away. I take the escalator network that connects the entire city.

Using a master key, I enter Choi Gangwu's apartment. It's like a completely empty hotel room. A television that takes up an entire wall, a bed, sofa, coffee table, desk, chair, closet— that's all. The only personal touches are a ceramic statue of the Virgin Mary and a family photograph on the desk. A boy who looks like Choi Gangwu as a child, his father, and a girl I assume is his sister. Unlike Choi Gangwu, who is good-looking but somehow lacking in some department, his sister looks like she may very well grow into a classic beauty. Curious, I search for her photo; I'm right.

I take a seat in the chair and look around at the empty apartment. Closing my eyes, I imagine Choi Gangwu here, sleeping, watching TV, catching up on work. I take a deep sniff of some of the clothes hanging in his closet. I try to absorb the existence of this man who has so suddenly popped into my life.

I can't just ignore him or let him get away with it. I have to determine what he's up to. And fast.

THE BUTTERFLY AND THE SPACE ELEVATOR

"He said his name was Dr. Sekewael. That's how I remember it," says Choi Gangwu.

I cross my arms and sit back. Choi Gangwu bows lower as he stares down at the desk. His worried expression looks real enough. If it isn't real it's acting, and he had no opportunity in his life to learn that kind of acting.

"His friends called him Zach. I think Sekewael was his family name. I don't know the people's names here very well."

"What did he say when he approached you?" I ask, trying to sound as neutral as possible.

"He said he was an entomologist. And asked if I liked butterflies."

"Do you?"

"Do I what?"

"Like butterflies."

"Yeah. But I don't collect them or anything. I can always look at collections in natural history museums. I like living butterflies. I'm a butterfly watcher. There are seventy-five species of butterflies in Patusan and forty-two of them live only on this island. I try to go butterfly watching when I can."

"A rare hobby."

"I grew up out in the country. I'm also shy so I don't have many friends. I like to watch insects. Especially butterflies. I wanted to become an entomologist but couldn't afford to. My family was poor, I needed to make a living as quickly as possible. But I wasn't a great student. I can't concentrate on subjects I'm not interested in. But I'm still pretty good at knowing a little bit of many things."

"You managed to score the second-highest entrance points for this company."

"My sister got sick. I was motivated. And the entrance procedures worked in my favor the year I applied. We were picked based only on ability."

"Your father had a bad experience with us. Why did you choose LK?"

"I wanted to prove myself. I said all this to the interviewer." His face, which had briefly lit up at the mention of butterflies, had settled into gloom. A face unable to hide one's worries, the kind of face LK does not like.

"He's good at his job," Choi Gangwu's team leader had said when I spoke to him earlier. "He works hard. Quick on the uptake when it comes to work. But not very social, he doesn't get along with his colleagues. He sits there for hours without saying a word and then says the one wrong thing, spoiling the atmosphere. Not a team player. He could've stayed in Youngwol and taken care of his sister while he worked from home, I don't know why he came all the way to Patusan."

"He can work from home?"

"Well, more like he's the kind of personnel whom we can make work from home. But I think he's rather ambitious. And he loves the space elevator. Knows lots of things about it beyond the scope of his duties. Oh, and quite a lepidopterist. Butterflies and the space elevator. As long as you love those two things, Patusan would be heaven, even for the worst anti-social person. Not exactly promotion material, though."

I clear my throat and readjust my pose. "This so-called Zachary Sekewael," I say to Choi Gangwu, "is a spy from the Patusan Liberation Front. Fortunately, you've behaved properly in every way. Not leaking any company secrets—"

"I don't know any to leak them," he says, ruining my delivery.

"More important, Sekewael doesn't know you've been found out. Which is why you're now an important asset to our External Affairs. How much are you willing to cooperate with the company?'

"But I'm not much of a spy. I don't even know where to begin. I'm a terrible talker, and hopeless in social situations."

"We're not asking you to play the Oscar-winning role of a lifetime. There's no danger, either. And if you help us, we'll transfer you to any division you want. What about the top floor? If you work there you can ride the spider and visit the station and counterweight. Have you been to space since you got here?"

The sight of Choi Gangwu's suddenly brightening face makes me smile inwardly. No, my friend, you're definitely not spy material.

After the interrogation, I ask him if he likes Thai food; he nods, more of a reflex than enthusiasm. I take my freshly caught bait to the window seat at Siam Sunset that I'd reserved two days ago; on a clear day you can see a third of the island and the very tip of Pala from there.

As we eat, I extract Choi Gangwu's story from him little by little. There are three meaningful things in his life: his sister, butterflies, and the space elevator. I understand the sister and the butterflies. But why the elevator? And why choose to transfer to Patusan? Had he always been interested in the elevator?

"Is it because your father's invention is being used here?" I ask carefully.

"Sort of, but I'm not sure anymore. In the beginning, I knew about it but that was it. I also knew that once the elevator is completed, all kinds of wonderful things will come true, from space travel to global climate control. But the moment I decided to go to LK Space, I suddenly had an interest in it. Like I opened a door and the ocean flooded in. I wish I had a better simile but I'm not great at that kind of thing."

"And now?"

"I love it as much as I love butterflies. Sometimes even more. I said this in the interviews, and they seemed to respond well. Do you think that's why they picked me?"

A little bit of alcohol unlocks all sorts of stories. From Konstantin Tsiolkovsky to Mika Vettel, the history of countless scientists and engineers involved in the space elevator, the history of Patusan, LK, the dazzling future ahead. He is so passionate that I feel as if I've stepped into one of those Korean Evangelical churches in an old film.

Something isn't right. Not the part about liking butterflies and the space elevator, that's not so unusual.

But when he talks about the space elevator, he turns into a different person. That dreamy look he has when he talks about butterflies disappears, and a cunning, devious person emerges. By the time he's wildly gesticulating in the air, criticizing LK's policies, he seems to have forgotten he's just an insignificant assistant to the higher-ranked engineers on the project.

I feel very strange. There's something familiar about this man's words and manners. But what?

HOW TO USE HUMAN BAIT

The real name of Zachary Sekewael, the infamous ZS, was Neberu O'Shaughnessy. Born in Pala, he has citizenship there as well as in Ireland and Sulaco. He has at least three identities, each with at least two nationalities. Some people don't have citizenship anywhere, and some have too many.

He has no interest in butterflies or space elevators. O'Shaughnessy is local staff of a company called Green Fairy, headquartered in Vientiane. The name of the company makes it sound like it sells liquor, but it's actually registered as a bodyguard agency. And indeed, that's what it looks like on the surface; underneath the façade, they're basically spies for hire. Industrial espionage mostly, but Green Fairy is not particular about its customers. The reason I know about them is that we used to be a client. We do these operations in-house now, but eight years ago things were very different.

It doesn't really change that much about what we know, however. The only new info is that we now know the Liberation Front is working with Green Fairy. The Front and O'Shaughnessy long ago lost their interest in this pitiful man. Anything I do from here on out is based solely on my personal curiosity. Right?

Wrong. Exactly four days after my interrogation of Choi Gangwu, a message arrives from him. Sekewael has returned to Patusan. They're due to meet the next day. What is he to do?

We've already calculated the Front's next steps. After the ambush at the Gondal Quarter, they would've reassessed their intelligence on us. Probably guessed that we knew about O'Shaughnessy and Choi Gangwu. The latter's value, practically nonexistent a moment ago, suddenly soars. They've realized that we can try to manipulate O'Shaughnessy through Choi Gangwu. Countless variables exist. For example, we could rehire Green Fairy right under the Front's nose. That may even be the Front's objective.

In this dim fog of possibilities, there is only one thing that's certain. Choi Gangwu has to accept the invitation.

I put together the official paperwork and call him in to External Affairs. Everyone in Patusan knows that the division is basically a corporate spy organization, and making up a stupid reason for bringing in a newbie techie like Choi Gangwu is just a waste of time, so I don't bother. For our sake, and for the Front's, I want to minimize the amount of artifice. When Choi Gangwu follows us out, someone taps on their desk and whistles a familiar tune. Theme song of an old British spy movie series that everyone has heard of but never seen.

My second-in-command, Miriam Andretta, gives Choi Gangwu the information he needs, compressed into a form that's a fourth of its original size. The conspiracies have taken on layers of late, and the deeper one goes, the flimsier the narrative becomes. But the amount of information Choi Gangwu needs for this mission hasn't changed. All he needs to do is not get his little head mixed up in suspicions and do exactly what we tell him to.

Miriam inserts a small earphone in his ear and attaches a

sticker camera and microphone to his hideous Hawaiian shirt. There's a way of using the Worm the company has installed in him, but there's no need to go through another person's brain to get this done. The advantage of seeing through the Worm is that the visual information is a bit more accurate, that's all. More important, it's better to allow a bit of distance when working with someone this inexperienced.

When we've finished preparing him, Choi Gangwu makes his way slowly down to the beach, taking countless escalators.

Miriam and I tail him at about one hundred meters, watching the screens in our peripheral vision that show us the sticker-camera view and information from HQ.

The island's CCTV and security drones have already confirmed Sekewael's location. Through the monitor screen, I study his profile, a man in a straw hat bought from a beach vendor, sitting on the sand and gazing at the ruins of the old city.

Choi Gangwu arrives and we get a shot of Neberu O'Shaughnessy through the sticker camera. The face of a con artist who wears inserts under his skin, enabling him to change his features in seconds. But once you have a fix on someone like that, it's easy to see through the disguise.

The two have stainless-steel cups of diabolo menthe in front of them as they start talking about butterflies. Sekewael came to the island because he had made an important discovery. A relative of his had died recently and left him some things, including a nineteenth-century Polish sailor's diary written in French, and his collection of butterflies, one of which had gone extinct in the twentieth century. The specimens weren't in great shape, but they were sufficient for the Patusan Museum of Natural History to extract the DNA and restore the species. Isn't that wonderful?

All lies. The face-reading program determines O'Shaughnessy is reciting lines from a script, acting. His eyes keep leaving Choi Gangwu's face and darting about, indicating that he knows we are watching. Occasionally he looks directly at the sticker camera, but there's no way of knowing if he's seen it or not.

O'Shaughnessy gets up, saying he will show Choi Gangwu the collection. Choi Gangwu follows. Absorbing the information pouring in from the two screens, I tail them. Now that I can't read their expressions, there are limits to how much I can predict their behavior. External Affairs AI lets me know where it thinks they're headed. A map comes up, and several yellow lines are drawn between them and the hotel O'Shaughnessy is staying at. It's not his usual hotel. There's no law against changing hotels, but everything must be regarded with suspicion. The yellow lines disappear one by one. Those remaining are not the shortest routes back to the hotel. I guess he wants to look at the ruins and the ocean a bit more. Not out of the question.

Suddenly, a yellow line beams into the water.

At the other end of it is an unmanned wingship from Pala.

An escape route.

Countless possibilities proliferate.

Until now, we'd assumed O'Shaughnessy thought that Choi Gangwu was our pawn. That we'd try to read each other's cards for a bit, play around with the bait we'd sent him, and let him go. This escape route does not fit the narrative.

It could be something other than an escape route. Just a ship waiting for some guests who wanted to take a walk on the beach. But if it was a getaway plan? What was O'Shaughnessy planning? A kidnapping? Considering the difference in strength between the two men and the fact that O'Shaughnessy knows we are watching, that's ridiculous. Also, that ship could never outrun the Patusan police.

As the yellow lines continue to disappear, the line for the escape route thickens. Now the two are walking down a breakwater where no one's around. The rational thing for me to do is wait. To wait and see what I can make of O'Shaughnessy's intentions.

"Run, you fool!" I shout, dashing toward them. At my words, Miriam doesn't know what to do except run along with me. Choi Gangwu stops, turns, and starts to run toward me. O'Shaughnessy is running behind him. He's holding something in his left hand—a short pipe, but clearly a weapon. No matter how we try to prevent guns on the island, we can't block the production of weapons using portable printers.

Choi Gangwu trips over a paving stone and flops absurdly on the ground. O'Shaughnessy jumps on Choi Gangwu's rear and raises the pipe.

I aim for his shoulder and shoot.

The two chrome needles pierce his triceps. Spasming, he falls to the ground and the pipe drops from his hand and rolls into the ocean.

Choi Gangwu gets up, unsteady on his feet. He looks shocked at this sudden burst of violence, and he's drooling from the left side of his mouth.

An explosion lights up the ocean. The wingship at the end of the yellow line has been incinerated. O'Shaughnessy screams.

Five seconds later, he stops as abruptly as he started. His left eye is suddenly bloodshot, bleeding.

Something has exploded in his brain.

THE FIRST INSPECTION

"A Worm extractor."

I shake the long metallic apparatus taken out of O'Shaugh-nessy's pocket and shake it in front of the three faces glaring at me through the screen.

"We also recovered the pipe that fell into the water. An electric gun with two bullets. Hastily assembled, but still effective. Ten seconds to shoot down Choi Gangwu with the pipe gun, and ten seconds to extract the Worm from him with this thing—twenty seconds in all. Our team didn't go on the embankment path because we didn't want to be caught. Which means, if he had finished the deed in thirty seconds, he could've made it to the wingship. Of course, getting away with it would've been impossible. But he might have had time to jet the extracted Worm at least off to Pala. Even if the final destination wasn't Pala and was somewhere else."

"That's all possible in twenty seconds?" asks Ross Lee. I press the extractor button to demonstrate. A mechanical viper with an arrow-shaped head darts out of the apparatus and snaps its jaws.

"I'm being generous when I say twenty seconds. Plunging

it into the left eye saves you fifteen of those seconds. Miriam tested it herself."

"Why on Earth would O'Shaughnessy go to that trouble? Gangwu is just a new employee at the bottom of the ladder."

"You're right. The company checked his Worm, and there's no information in there that the Liberation Front or anyone else would possibly want. We checked to see if a second Worm had been inserted, but there was nothing. I don't know why O'Shaughnessy did what he did, but the information he acted on was false.

"The problem is that we don't know how they came upon such flawed intelligence. I think it's possible they thought Choi Gangwu wanted to avenge his father. But that's different from thinking he had anything in his Worm worth stealing."

"Isn't there a chance that Choi is some spy hired by another company?" Han Suhyun cuts in.

"He was vetted very thoroughly. No doubt because of the father situation. For an industrial spy to pass that test would be difficult, but not impossible. Still, did Choi Gangwu ever have an opportunity to come in contact with important assets while at Patusan? No. More than anything else, he simply did not have the time to be trained as a spy before he entered the company. Unless they made a clone of him and switched him out, like in a television show. Do you want me to check that, just in case? I will if you insist. This situation calls for extreme measures, short of killing him."

"Why did that Sekewael or O'Shaughnessy or whoever he is take on this mission? When he had no chance of escape." This was Mayor Nia Abbas. She didn't really seem to care that much about the proceedings, but she must've been impatient to hear her voice among the men's.

"I think he was being manipulated by the Worm. That's not

science fiction anymore. Of course, simply installing a Worm
isn't enough. He'd have to have been thoroughly primed psy-
chologically. So that a button pressed from the Worm could
start off a preprogrammed behavior script.

"That's as much as I know about it. Maybe a Worm could do
more now, but not much more. In other words, regardless of
whether O'Shaughnessy was successful or not, the bomb in his
brain would've killed him.

"The question remains whether he was killed by the Liberation Front or by someone else, but my money is on the latter.
Judging by the Front's reactions, I don't think they predicted
this situation, either. It seems they'd sent O'Shaughnessy on
a mission different from this one and he'd gone berserk. The
Front is just a tool being controlled by all kinds of different
powers anyway. They can do any crazy thing and it wouldn't
seem out of character. But this time, someone has acted without informing the Front.

"Our next step? We're going to talk to the Green Fairy people. They've lost a man themselves, so I'm sure they don't feel
great about it. There's some possibility of this being their doing,
but I think not. From what I know, they're not the kind of outfit
that treats their workers like this. I think if we put some more
personnel on the ground and trace O'Shaughnessy's recent
activities, we'll uncover more clues.

"As far as our man Choi Gangwu—he consented to adding
a surveillance device in his Worm and phone. We can now tell
where he is at any time, and it's impossible for him to contact
anyone on the outside without our knowing. Not that he con-
tacts anyone other than his sister."

After some meaningless chatter, the trio on the screen disappears. Above them reappears a projection of a hideous oil
painting depicting Yellowstone Park before the Great Explo-

sion. It grates my aesthetic sense whenever I lay eyes on it, but I never change this painting. I need something uncomfortable to stimulate me.

Sinking into the sofa, I look around me. Beige walls, a window with a view of the ocean through the trees, a front door, closets, and a brown door leading to the bedroom. A sight that hasn't changed in the last seven years. A space where time does not accumulate. Unless something peculiar happens, it will go on looking like this for the next seven years.

I verify Choi Gangwu's location. He's left the hospital and is now in front of his apartment. A smaller space, but not that different from my own. Although it now houses one additional item since my breaking and entering: a wood carving in the shape of an egg, with writhing naked bodies intertwined like snakes. This vulgar item, about twelve centimeters high, is by the bed. It is the item that Choi Gangwu brought back from Damon Chu's locker at H & H that day, along with a roll of bills amounting to eight thousand credits. Nothing else. I can't quite call it stealing. I think he was testing his strength.

I don't know what to make of it. By every standard, Choi Gangwu is a simpleton. He speaks simply, thinks simply, and hides nothing. Look at how easily he passed HR's polygraph. Normally someone at my level wouldn't even know he existed. But this simpleton of simpletons suddenly enters LK Space, second from the top, and is toying around with a secret known only to me and the dead president. Could it be that he also knows who was manipulating the fake Dr. Sekewael?

He may escape the notice of humans, but there's a strange fog of abnormality about him that can't quite escape AI pattern recognition.

A ghost, I think. Or something, controlling his every move. But if it's not in his Worm, where is it hiding?

DATE WITH THE GREEN WITCH

There was a time when Pala was known as the "Outhouse of Patusan." And seeing as how Patusan once processed its garbage and waste products on the island before it built its own facilities, the moniker wasn't entirely incorrect. But in that previous era, Pala had provided 30 percent of the food consumed on Patusan, a number that has now climbed to 50 percent. You'd think that would warrant a new nickname, but making them up must be a bothersome enterprise.

I am looking down at the city from a suite on the twenty-first floor of the Fairmont. Factories that process rice and other produce, fruit, salmon, codfish, protein powder, and the like are arranged in a chessboard formation, a nuclear fusion plant at the center. Pala's northern shore, lined with municipal and residential buildings, as well as its western shore, where most of the Patusan-born populace lives, are out of eyeshot. Patusan is closer than Pala's own western shore from here.

Her face as elongated and sorrowful as one in a Modigliani painting, Sumac Graaskamp sits with her back straight on the small wooden chair behind her desk and reads the police file on Neberu O'Shaughnessy. Graaskamp is a VP of Green Fairy and is known in the industry as the "Green Witch"—she takes care of all the company's affairs except its official bodyguard work. Which is another way of saying that she's in charge of all the shady deaths and disappearances that point back to Green Fairy in one way or another. Finding the link between these mysteries and her company, however, is generally tiresome work, and it's therefore rare that anyone seeking their services would trouble themselves by thinking about the people who've died or disappeared in Green Fairy's hands.

Green Fairy submitted the perfect alibi to the police this morning: *O'Shaughnessy had been assigned bodyguard detail to certain agents affiliated with the Patusan Liberation Front. No matter what your politics, they, too, deserve safety. Not even we know why O'Shaughnessy would act as a spy for the Front. We had nothing to do with this affair. We've long since cut ties with the Front.*

The police didn't believe everything they said, but their story checked out, down to the last detail.

"We didn't kill O'Shaughnessy."

I could hear her firm voice from behind my back.

"It doesn't matter if you don't believe me, Mac. We don't treat our own employees like that. Especially O'Shaughnessy. It would be a waste to erase him like that. He was good at his job, but it's more than that. Do you have any idea how much we invested in his body and brain? His last insertion surgery was only a week ago. We're going to salvage as much as possible before he's completely disintegrated, but our losses are pretty steep here."

I ask, "Do you think someone fiddled with him during his last surgery?"

"We're talking about a field operative's augmentation. Do you think we're just going to hire someone off the street for that? And this incident goes far beyond simply hacking some-

one's Worm. This has been going on for at least a year now, I'm
sure of it. They're not the savviest, but they're flush with money
and time."

"And you're sure it's not the Liberation Front?"

"Come on, you know it's not them. This doesn't fit the narrative of anyone we know. At least no one Green Fairy is aware of.
You really don't have a clue who it might be? Is that employee
of yours really as middling and inconsequential as this report
makes him out to be?"

"Yes, he is."

Graaskamp narrows her eyes and points her skinny right
index finger at me.

"I smell a rat, Mac. Something strange is going on. Don't
think we're going to let this slide without satisfying our own
curiosity. And I bet we're not the only ones who've caught on to
the stink. If you want to keep protecting your little friend, you
better choose sides fast."

"And if that little friend does happen to be extremely important, and I ask for your help, would you step in?" I watch her
face carefully.

"I don't know, Mac. Maybe not like this. If I give you something, you've got to give something back. And the only thing
we consider worth receiving is intel. Can you give me that?"

I don't answer. Graaskamp grins, as if this were the response
she expected, gets up, and walks to her door, which she opens
for me. Along the length of the hall two pairs of guards' eyes
follow me as I drift into the elevator.

Once I am out of the hotel, I walk toward the harbor. The
sun is setting. A group of skinny teenagers, who look about
fifteen years old, are fishing on a raft assembled from Univer-
sal Blocks. I bet you anything they're Patusans living on the
western coast. When Pala became Patusan's food factory, the

few professional fishers changed their jobs or left for Taprobana, even farther from Tamoé. Anyone fishing for food from
these waters is a native Patusan. A third of whom have failed to
assimilate into the Pala system. They even use their own separate electricity—provided to them through seven tidal generators that stretch into the ocean like squid legs.

Most of them have some connection to the Liberation Front,
but it's hard to say if they're actually involved. The Front, after
all, is tough to pin down. They have no common objective,
and there's too much outside interference. The Patusan settle-
ment on Pala has nothing to do with the roots of the Liberation
Front. What binds them isn't greed or whatever vague version
of patriotism one might credit them with, but stubbornness
and romanticism. A group of eccentrics proving it's possible
to survive independently, without the help of a conglomerate-
corporate system, in a world that's been totally changed since
the Great Explosion. They aren't even the first group of this
stripe to settle on Pala.

LK's President Han abhorred their ideals. Living in harmony
with nature was a meaningless fantasy, even before the Great
Explosion. When it comes to nature, humanity has no choice
but to be destructive. The best thing humanity can do for
nature is to sequester itself from nature. In his youth, President
Han was obsessed with perfect arcologies. With the advent of
LK Space his focus moved to skyhooks and the space elevator,
but that didn't mean his previous interest had disappeared. The
great structure of Patusan City, as it flowed down the mountain
like waterfalls, was itself a single building, and theoretically
could survive as a self-sufficient city should it become isolated.
We chose to off-load some of the city's essentials to Pala for
purely diplomatic reasons.

And in President Han's final days, we did our best to take

care of the Patusan population in Pala. Giving them a direct payoff would have been out of the question, but what we could do was give them jobs in Pala's factories and anonymously donate tidal generators to the community at large. The idea at the time was that they needed to be satisfied with their lives on Pala in order for business to run unimpeded. Whether or not we still believe this, I don't know. The Liberation Front, having lost their foundation of real, living members, has become an even more amorphous and unpredictable player. There was no safe way for us to disband them. All we could do was admit that people, as a group, are not as easy to control as we once thought.

Five minutes before its departure, I board a ferry. As the ferries between Pala and Patusan run on guiderails, they're basically floating trains. The few passengers are all on deck, watching the sun go down behind Pala Mountain.

The Green Witch is right. Choi Gangwu is simply too odd to ignore. The myriad forces that have their eyes on Patusan will smell blood and swarm the island like flies. The ones who think they know what secret Choi Gangwu is hiding will make haste. Would that dim-witted bastard survive amid the chaos?

And would I?

YOU ALWAYS THOUGHT THAT.
EVEN WHEN I TOLD YOU IT WASN'T SO

Choi Gangwu and I are sitting in an office I've borrowed for
External Affairs. Miriam, who'd been with us until a moment
ago, has left to have it out with Security. Normally she's cool
and calm to a fault, but it's a different story when Rex Tamaki
is involved. They'd been lovers for a year and enemies for these
past two, and she sincerely believes this man is distorting
information just to make her life hell. Maybe she's right. Not
because he has feelings for her but because he just enjoys making people's lives hell.

Aside from a table and five chairs, the room is empty. The
view out the windows, as on Patusan, is of trees and ocean. The
only difference is the elevation.

Choi Gangwu, meanwhile, is fine, having gotten away with
only a hairline fracture to his left wrist. Considering everything he went through two days before, his dazed expression
and the jittery way he's shaking his left leg are understandable.

"That butterfly was real," he says.

"What?"

"The Polish sailor's diary, too. I called the police just to make
sure, and they said the diary and butterfly box were really in the
hotel. I sent some museum people over. Once the legal prob-

lems are sorted out, the butterflies will end up in a museum. That's what I was told."

I nod my head, not giving it too much thought. Where DNA from an extinct butterfly ends up is none of my concern. Although it does impress me a little, this thoroughness, coming from a dead person. Using real props to construct a lie that needed to last just a couple of minutes. Or maybe it hadn't been a complete lie? Did O'Shaughnessy, in his impersonation of Sekewael, develop a sincere interest in butterflies? Was there something substantial behind this lepidopteran bond?

His jittery left leg comes to a halt. Choi Gangwu stares down at his two hands resting meekly on the table and speaks.

"Would I, would I really get to be on the top floor?"

How to answer this? The truth is, I'd seriously thought of sending him there. Disguising him as someone more important than he really was, playing along with the Liberation Front's game. But O'Shaughnessy had gone haywire and the plan came to naught. Choi Gangwu was still an important asset to me, but whether I kept that particular promise was a separate matter.

Not that there was any reason *not* to send him up. From there you could see the cable and spiders up close, and feel closer to space, but it's not like that's the only place where important things happen. The symbolic meanings behind its name and altitude are greater than the sum of the elevator. To use an expression the Koreans are always using, it's all a matter of one's feelings. And there were numerous excuses I could invent to justify sending a low-tier employee like Choi Gangwu up the elevator.

What's truly valuable is the island itself. No one thought so at first. A platform built on a bit of neutral, empty ocean seemed to be enough, no need for a land base. But LK Space had bigger ambitions. President Han wanted the elevator to grow. More cables, more spiders. He wanted factory infrastructure to support it. He needed an island, and he happened to hear of one with a failed and abandoned resort.

"Our operation is over," I say to Choi Gangwu. "We didn't know this was how it would end, but that's the way it is. You're no longer needed here now. But we do expect there to be attempts on your life, so we can't just send you off. We need to figure out what happened, and in the meantime you need to stay under our protection. Let's talk about the top floor once we sort this all out. I'm sure it will be possible, if you really want it. There's room. Do you want to go there that badly?"

He nods.

"Even if we'd never encouraged you in the first place?"

"The top floor has always been my goal. Even if you hadn't come around, I would've applied to go up."

"You don't have to be assigned there. Why not just go up as a tourist?"

"It's not enough. Some really incredible things are happening up there."

This is followed by an astonishingly long and rapturous ode to the top floor. A slew of technical terms, spinning and hopping and prancing about. Visions of the technology, words painting a vivid picture. Not that I understand half of it, or am convinced in any way, but I do find the passion and articulateness of his praise impressive. More so because this doesn't fit my idea of the man Choi Gangwu. His passion for the space elevator is very different from his ponderous and profound interest in butterflies. More than anything else, it's the rich vocabulary that's being utilized here.

In other words, this isn't Choi Gangwu. This is something that didn't exist until a few years ago. Inside the butterfly lover before me hides something alien and unfamiliar. The same thing that pulled Choi Gangwu into LK Space. The thing the people who controlled Sekewael/O'Shaughnessy had thought was inside Choi Gangwu's Worm but wasn't.

I invite Choi Gangwu to dinner again. This time, we travel in the opposite direction—down from the new city and into the ruins of the sunken city, where the Indigenous population lives, in villages along the crescent-shaped strip of land. A world where the smells of dead fish, pungent spices, and sweat assault the nostrils. With our teeth, we rip off chunks of fish flesh and slightly charred scales, and we wash it all down with beer. When two moths fly into the yellow bulb overhead, the entomologist in Choi Gangwu is revived. I listen to his ensuing lepidoptery lecture. A completely different speaker from the one a few hours before. Shy, slow, a bit lazy, chill, ordinary. And the moonshine beer heating his blood isn't enough to account for the change.

I prop his stumbling body up as we exit the restaurant. Briefly I consider calling a capsule taxi but decide to walk instead.

We stare up at the shining new city that seems to hover above the abandoned ruins below. With the glow-in-the-dark aquatic insects and the accompanying full moon, the sight before us becomes excessively beautiful, verging on tacky.

Somewhere in the village, harpsichord music is pouring from a speaker. Everything important that happens on Patusan is associated with a short theme composed by Fatima Bellasco. Endless variations on the theme are created by AI, music that sweeps over the island like waves. Once you get used to it, you can tell what's going on around you just by the music playing through your Worm or the speakers. The same way an experienced music lover can follow the plot of a Wagner opera without knowing a word of German.

The music playing now is familiar even to first-time visitors. It's the theme for the spiders. Five days ago, Andrei Kostomaryov's space development company ALYSSA launched their Jupiter-bound ship, *Holst,* carrying four passengers, using the very elevator that is now on its way back with samples of meteorites. Between the two laser beams shooting up from the mountaintops descends the blinking orange star of a spider.

Behold, the fruits of fifteen years of labor. In the earlier days of the space elevator, a robot the size of a suitcase grabbed hold of a cable descending from the sky, then spent twenty-five days crawling up to orbital altitude. That same trip now takes only two days. Even without the kinds of things that SF writers like to imagine, such as linear motors. Once you start following the objectives set by people from the past, you're bound to stumble upon a simpler, more convenient technology. When AI began participating in creative tasks, the speed of change and diversity of thought increased exponentially. President Han once said that the role of human beings, in the near future, would be to boost the machine civilization that's on its way.

I hear an inebriated tongue trying to form human words.

"What was that?" I ask.

Choi Gangwu puts on a stupid grin and repeats himself. "You always thought that. Even when I told you it wasn't so."

THE FAINT FOOTPRINTS OF A GHOST

"You always thought that. Even when I told you it wasn't so."

I remember these words. Not because they have some important meaning but because of the opposite: they have almost no meaning, are just a throwaway comment. Or at least, as far as I can remember.

I don't recall their context. What I do recall is President Han Junghyuk's laughing face as he looks into my puzzled eyes. When I ask him again what he means, President Han merely repeats his words, chuckling. Annoying as it is to be laughed at for no reason, he's the head of the LK Group, so I keep my mouth shut.

That was ten years ago. My Korean, which I'd learned through the Worm, was still clunky. Speaking Korean made me feel like the surface membrane of my personality was separating from my body—making me very anxious. This happened with languages I'd learned through other means, too, but anyone who learned a language using one of the Worm's earlier models suffered through particularly acute versions of this side effect.

The other thing about the Worm's language education system is that it creates ghosts. Figures that hover in your peripheral vision, stumbling along the borders of several languages, muttering strange spells. After the funeral, one of my ghosts started talking in President Han's voice.

When Choi Gangwu said what he said, I heard two voices at once. Choi Gangwu's, and the congruently superimposed voice of my ghost. For a moment I thought I'd misheard—that it had been the ghost's voice alone. But no. The words had been spoken from Choi Gangwu's mouth in Choi Gangwu's voice. Choi Gangwu speaking Han Junghyuk's lines.

I wondered if it was a code of some sort. But that couldn't be. Choi Gangwu seems unaware that his recent words have any meaning. Clearly it was something stashed in his mind, taking advantage of his alcohol-addled state to emerge and make itself known.

Something. Something that carries Han Junghyuk's memories.

When I escort him to his apartment, Choi Gangwu doesn't seem to notice me staring at his family photos and the obscene wooden egg. He says a halfhearted goodbye and disappears into the bathroom. I close the door behind me as I leave.

On the escalator, I'm lost in thought. The puzzle pieces in my mind are clicking into place. This schlub, who had no real hobbies or interests except lepidoptery until a few years ago, suddenly becomes a fanatic of the space elevator and enters LK Space with the second-highest marks, a feat that included not only acing the written exam but impressing the highly skeptical live interviewers.

The easiest and simplest answer to the question of how this happened is that a Worm containing President Han's memories is in Choi Gangwu's brain. Even if the only Worm in his head is the one the company implanted there, with nothing special to it. But there's just no way the dead president's memories and mind, and all the conspiracies they're wrapped up in, could be discovered so easily. Let's assume there's something shrewder afoot here, something that managed to pass through our rigorous inspection process, and forget for the time being how it managed to evade detection.

How could the dead president's memories still be around? From what I know, he had at least four Worms. Two were for his Alzheimer's. There are much easier ways of treating Alzheimer's, but the president took it as a new technological challenge. By the time of his death, Han Junghyuk's mind was much more widely dispersed than a normal person's. We're not simply talking about the ability to store select memories in the cloud.

When he died, Han Junghyuk's data—aside from the instances preselected while he was alive—was destroyed according to the Privacy Protection Act. At least, that's what we believed. The president himself had ordered this, and the Han Junghyuk we knew was not someone who did things halfway. But our beliefs were nothing more than assumptions. We just weren't interested in the private data he left behind; the important data had been transferred to the company's AI already. LK, to this day, is steered by the ambitions of a dead man. Ross Lee or Han Suhyun can't even begin to alter its direction. So why should we care about this hypothetical private data of Han Junghyuk's, which may or may not exist? Why should we suspect that this data was not destroyed?

We simply don't know him very well. Because of his carefully curated image, we can't imagine Han Junghyuk as a normal, living, breathing human being. But everyone has secrets. No one can ever be known completely to another person. There may have been some hidden thing that Han Junghyuk had wanted to leave behind. And that thing might be more important than anything we could imagine. And it could very well be in Choi Gangwu's brain. And someone who knows this might be trying to get to Choi Gangwu.

So was it mere coincidence that the words only I can remember had issued forth from his lips in that moment? Is it another coincidence that I'm the only person in the company who has a personal interest in Choi Gangwu? And that I saved his life?

I consider the position I'm in now. To the company, all I am is some personal hire by the late President Han. Before the old man died, he had put a bit of a safety mechanism in place for me, but it won't last forever. Once someone learns my real name, nationality, and what my face looked like before the surgery, this safety mechanism is kaput. Ross Lee won't care about my identity one way or another, but Han Suhyun—he's a different story.

If the thing that's inside Choi Gangwu's brain is really a part of the president, that could be my lifeline. Choi Gangwu is irrelevant to the company's official processes, but he might be a tool for carrying out important tasks, among which is guarding the president's people.

Once I return to my apartment, I look through my intel on Choi Gangwu. Miriam has already gone over it and found nothing. But that was before I knew there was something there to be found. I have an inkling of what patterns and routes I need to look for now. I search his movements and his personal emails and messages.

A little while later, I suddenly recall a message the tracking AI had put seven yellow stars next to, a deleted spam email from two years ago.

Want a job at LK Group, Chaeseong Group, TG Systems, or Pinto Space? Safety guaranteed, "almost" legal. Overcome your fate at a low price!

"Almost" legal. I grin. Not bad for bait, I must say. I've used it myself several times, I should know. And clearly Choi Gangwu took the bait himself. There are traces of his having clicked the link. It's understandable. An easy trap to fall into if you've applied to work at LK Space multiple times, almost out of habit, and if you also happen to be too lazy to have invested in your future. When you've got nothing, you've got nothing to lose.

Who else might've fallen for this? I look it up and learn that the scammers have already been caught—two arrests. More honest con artists than I would've thought. They weren't just going to run away with the money, they were going to actually surgically inject biobots to help the applicants cheat at exams. The robots they built could live in the brain for about two weeks and were hard to pick up on scans. The perps were techies who'd been fired from LK Robotics, and once they were out on probation LK rehired them. Which isn't as strange as it sounds. LK often hires criminals like these to ensure the protection of its corporate secrets. These two apparently are being paid handsome salaries to come up with gadgets at some in-house research center. I have no idea what they're making, but I can't help envying their good luck.

I look at the list of their victims. Twelve of them. All Choi Gangwu's age or thereabouts. Young, handsome, not very clever, with a certain irresponsible look that seems baked into their faces since birth.

Oh, about that. They're all men.

WHERE THE PICTURE OF THE
DISAPPEARED BUTTERFLIES IS

"Do you know that film, *North by Northwest*?"

"I think I've heard of it. A classic?"

"Alfred Hitchcock, twentieth century. Not strange that you haven't seen it. This is the story. An adman named Roger O. Thornhill is mistaken for a man named George Kaplan at a hotel. Which almost gets him killed, and he's taken for a murderer. So Thornhill tries to track down the real Kaplan himself, but it turns out Kaplan is a made-up figure created by the American government. He has a name and some belongings but no body."

"All right, so?"

"This guy is our George Kaplan."

The room we're in hasn't been used in almost four years, but with a robot coming around to clean it twice a week, it's relatively neat inside. There's just the right amount of lived-in disarray, and even a hint of bachelor pad musk, courtesy of an engineered scent in the air purifier.

Choi Gangwu looks at me with a stupid expression. I don't need the Worm to tell me it's faked. The muscles of his face are rigid and his eyelids tremble. A face that tells the truth even when it lies.

"The owner of this home is named Damon Chu. He's got more of a paper trail than I do. Because he has a nationality, and his DNA biometrics are on file. But no body. He's a being designed to implode forever if the company needs him to. That's why no one should have been in this room. The fake fingerprints the cleaning robot leaves behind should be the only fingerprints present here. And if there are other fingerprints? How do we explain that? Anyone who knows the location and door code of this apartment, and is capable of breaking through our security, that person would know they're not supposed to leave fingerprints in here. So why did they?"

I shut the door and walk toward the elevator. Choi Gangwu follows me without saying a word. Once we're out of the building, we walk along the banks of the Brunel. In eight hundred meters we come across H & H Storage. Huge shipping containers painted colorfully with manhwa characters are stacked on top of each other like LEGO pieces.

I retrieve an old-fashioned metal key from the front office and we walk up the steel steps to Damon Chu's container on the third floor. Inside, the air is dry and smells of iron. I switch on the light and look through the contents. Aside from the vulgar egg and a cashbox, nothing seems to be missing. I take out the Tintin poster signed by Hergé and put it in the aluminum case I'd brought with me.

Dusting off an ebony chair with two dragons carved into its back, I sit down and ask, "Why did you take the statue? Does it have some kind of special meaning?"

He replies, "It was pretty."

"You like that kind of thing?"

"I suppose."

"You suppose? And I suppose you know how a newbie hire, who hasn't even been on the job for a year, finds out about a fake persona that not a single soul in External Affairs is aware of and then makes his way into this secret container?"

"I just wanted to see something."

"What something?"

"Whether the something I knew was correct." He shrugs and looks up from the spot on the floor he'd locked his gaze on.

"When did you learn about Damon Chu?"

"About two months ago. Yeah, that's right."

"How?"

"I just remembered his face. I thought he was a real person at first. A relative of President Han's. Their eyes and mouths look similar. But then, after that, I remembered his name. The addresses of his apartment and this storage locker and what was inside the locker. That's when I started feeling sure Damon Chu was not a real person, and that it would be all right for me to come here. That was the something I wanted to see."

"Whether that vulgar egg was here?"

"No. This."

Choi Gangwu strides toward the stack of twelve paintings in their protective cases, leaning against each other in a corner. The lights come on and he draws one of the frames out of the stack. It's a painting of butterflies, about two meters tall. Seven butterflies hover around a flower blooming by a creek, a crescent moon in the top right corner.

"Jang Soon-ok's *Butterflies Under the Moon*. A twentieth-century painter. She did the most beautiful butterfly paintings, but was never famous. Maybe because she was a woman, or half Japanese, or painted only butterflies. Or people just weren't that interested. I don't know. This painting hung in some municipal museum in Incheon before it was stolen. I've only seen low-resolution photographs of it, taken in the twentieth century. But I remembered it was here. And when I came to check, it really was. It's been well maintained, but it belongs back in that museum."

The painting rattled as he slid it back into place. Choi Gangwu, who'd looked despondent while being dragged from Patusan to Bandar Seri Begawan, finally perked up a little. What a funny little comic book hero he was: one who obtained strength through proximity to butterflies.

"You began remembering all that two months ago?"

"It's been a year. You probably know by now that I had a procedure? I was convinced I'd be found out right away. Because my CV made no sense, even to me. The people who operated on me were arrested right after they performed my procedure. Everyone else they operated on had their employment canceled. I shouldn't have been an exception, but no one came for me. I thought they'd reject me after the interview, at least, but that didn't happen, either."

"Why, do you think?"

"Well, I gave a good interview. I kept spouting things I had no idea I knew. And I had all this confidence I didn't normally have. I aced it. All thanks to the biobot those con artists put in my head. It died in two weeks and the body disintegrated, but it altered a part of my brain while it was alive. That part is basically functioning as a Worm. A brain inside my brain, thinking its own thoughts.

"But why was I spared? I've thought long and hard about it. I did pass that test. A test that culled twelve people out of thirteen, but I passed it. And that's why I also passed the interview. I did well, for sure, but there was something helping me, something beyond the opinion of the interviewers themselves. There was someone who really, really wanted me to join LK Space."

VISIT FROM A GUARDIAN ANGEL

"Everything I told you earlier is true. My father was involved in some unsavory business with LK. You might say he killed himself over it. But to exact revenge on LK? I'd never even imagine it. That would be like exacting revenge on a god. And I simply didn't like my father that much. He was a cold man, lost in his own world. Maybe if he'd involved himself in the lives of others he'd still be alive today. Wanting to be treated like a genius inventor, in this day and age, really? Even Thomas Edison or Nikola Tesla, whose photographs hung on the walls in his lab, were not lone wolves.

"It was out of sheer stubbornness and fear that I kept applying to work at LK Space. I wasn't ready to face the outside world. Earning some spending money through microlabor and chasing down butterflies wasn't a bad way to live. But for the rest of my life? That's terrifying. I needed a way to justify my laziness. And what's a better excuse than challenging myself to work for the company that's said to have killed my father? It was such a good excuse that I believed in it with all my heart. But if that was it, I would've applied just once and moved on with my life.

"I had no intention of taking the hiring exam for the third time. For one thing, like I said, I wasn't making all that bad a living as it was. Microlabor was the perfect kind of work for a person like me, a jack-of-all-trades with a short attention span. Sometimes I made three or four times what I make now. My uncle had a job open in his shop in Youngwol, and I was able to take it. My sister was still sick so I needed money. But even that would be taken care of once I started working with my uncle.

"When I got the spam message, I ignored it at first. Two meaningless failures were more than enough. But the confidence in the message caught my attention. And I felt this strange sensation—a *click*—like the pieces of my life were falling into place. How can I explain it? Maybe it was like being a gambler, convinced that this time around is the one? Or like the author of my life story had dropped a symbol, some kind of foreshadowing.

"So I went to Kaesong and met up with the people who had sent the message. They looked almost like twins, and were about my age, but they weren't actually Korean, or even from the same country. I think part of it was that they both used the same awkward Korean, picked up from the Worm their Korean company had provided.

"They said they had once worked at the LK Robotics research center in Suwon, south of Seoul. On a very particular kind of biobot, one that could transfer whatever information you wanted to a living brain. They said they'd been fired for some bullshit reason and the company had no idea about these biobots yet. They'd already done experiments on them using their own bodies and were looking for other test subjects. And who better to experiment on than me, some lazy, no-talent wannabe trying to land a job at a big company? All they required was a minimal fee, one that even I could afford. Small enough for me to think of it as an expensive lottery ticket, which I could throw away if it didn't pan out. It ended up being the gamble of my dreams.

"The operation went off without complications. Quicker than the Worm implantation the company would administer later on, with no side effects like tinnitus or a narrowed field of vision. Just a little bit of delay with setting the time for the bug to die. The two visited my room regularly, assisting with the data transfer from the bug to my brain.

"It was a strange experience. Not like information being fed into the brain subconsciously, like over the Worm. As bits of information came alive in my brain, one by one, they linked with each other into a web that wrapped itself around my consciousness. Little by little I absorbed the information and made it mine. But the web remained long after the biobot died. A little scary. Though reassuring. Like having a guardian angel to advise me and prevent me from making mistakes.

"Taking the company entrance exam was like flying. Because I'd already tried it twice, I knew how it would go, first the written portion then the mental stability test. But this time I saw things I never would've seen before. Something like my perspective widening, and the whole process running slower than usual? When I got the second-highest score, I was genuinely surprised. That there could be anyone else who had scored higher than I had.

"The problem now was the interview. The duo who sold me the bug had by then been arrested. I saw them on the news. With the former clients being caught one by one, the entire incident had become the talk of the town. People were asking each other, Can we really say that using technology to get ahead is cheating? If it were allowed, what would it mean to select for talented individuals? The police didn't come for me and the duo never mentioned my name. Stressed and relieved at the same time, I went into the interview.

"There were six interviewers. Three women, three men. All wearing virtual masks, making them appear identical. I could only guess their genders and ages through their voices and words. They asked me about my father, and I had prepared the best answer I could imagine. I wouldn't even have cared if they didn't accept it, because I never could have thought up anything better.

"It was after that question that the weird thing happened. Someone asked about the space elevator, and I began the reply I'd rehearsed. But as I spoke, a realization came over me. Or better yet, a kind of tunnel formed between me and my guardian angel, and the most intoxicating emotion poured through that passage. The space elevator was no longer a combination of data and planning. It was an object of love. I loved that thin thread connecting Earth and space with a force that was driving me out of my mind. Like Romeo's love for Juliet, like Dante's for Beatrice. I started in on a long rant about the space elevator, and that rant was in a language of love. It may have been a little over the top. The company needs technicians, not fetishists. But I think my speech went a long way in easing their suspicions.

"I was ecstatic to have passed the exam. Completely ecstatic. Not just because I'd finally managed to enter LK Space but because I'd fallen in love with someone or other.

"Yes, 'someone or other.' I was slowly coming to grips with this as I left the exam site. My love for the space elevator didn't exist on its own. It somehow connected me to the love for a persona, a persona not necessarily linked to a human being. The space elevator was my connection to a someone or other.

"But who? I detected it was something feminine. Not necessarily a woman, but something like a woman. It was difficult to imagine it in any other form. Something to do with the form of the love I was feeling. If the object of my love had been a man, the texture and shape of my love would've been different.

"At first, I tried to simply enjoy the emotion. Because to feel it was more than enough. And now I was busy. I got to live overseas for the first time in my life after getting this job. It was also the first time since graduating from college that I had a real adult job, which made me anxious about surviving.

"My job was fun and also boring. For one thing, I loved Patusan from the start. I loved the perfect arcology LK had constructed, and the ruins, and the butterflies. And more than anything else, the space elevator. The work was fun, too. I was shuttled all over the place during my probationary period, and I loved anything and everything about the elevator. But I didn't get along with others, and my coworkers didn't like me. They still don't. They think I'm a braggart, an eccentric, not a team player. Some people whispered behind my back that I was a nepotistic hire, but what could I do? What point did fairness have in this place? I was the top expert on the space elevator. Did it matter all that much how I came upon my knowledge?

"I fell deeper and deeper into my own world. Just a year before, that world was very simple. Butterflies, my sister, my daydreams. But now something had infiltrated that world and was slowly expanding its territory. Something passionate and domineering, overpowering me in my hesitancy and weakness. It kept forcing me to do things, to feel things. I was scared of it, but seduced by its strength. A completely foreign lifestyle had taken me over. As I accepted these changes, I tried not to forget the man I was. Fortunately, Patusan was a butterfly paradise. As these two worlds collided, my experiences grew richer and richer.

"But there was also a kind of emptiness. The 'woman.' The love I'd inherited, for someone who may or may not exist, who was probably a woman. I couldn't recall her face. Can you imagine how frustrating that was, to have no clue whom I felt this love for?

"My first attempt at relief was to try to re-create the woman's appearance. First I used drawing. Then a montage program. But the results were always the same, some variation of a pretty woman. She might as well have been a composite of my personal taste, nothing to do with memory. Just re-creating her appearance wouldn't do. I needed to know something more.

"Oddly enough, fragments of that 'something more' were scattered all over Patusan. This city is not just a growth of machinery and architecture. It contains countless personal memories and emotions. And just being here made me feel them. Only I couldn't express them in specific words or images.

"The first piece of evidence came after I'd been here for three months. I was waiting along with a bunch of other new hires for the space elevator to come back with samples from the top floor, collected by the *Haebaragi 23,* from its rendezvous with the Abelonas-Viola Comet. We weren't there just for that. Whenever the elevator arrived, it would take some of the new employees up to the top on the way back. It gave them a chance to understand the workings of the company.

"The elevator arrived, to the tune of that theme song they made for it, and its doors opened. We unloaded the crates the scientists had packed at the top floor and put them on the cart. Some old guy—the leader, I guess—looked at us and said, 'Do any of you know what this is? Star stuff.'

"'Star stuff.' What a cliché. But the moment he said it, a very specific memory came to mind. A woman whose face I could not see, speaking in a voice I couldn't place: 'Look, Mr. Gildong. Star stuff.'

"Whoever's memory this was, they loved that woman.

"I immediately searched the name Gildong. Nothing came up. Maybe it was a nickname. Hong Gildong or Ko Gildong. It had to be Hong Gildong—after the mythical Korean figure. But why Hong Gildong? Famous for appearing in the east one moment, appearing in the west the next? No. Famous for being an illegitimate bastard—that was it. And who was more of an illegitimate bastard on the island of Patusan than Han Junghyuk? Was he not the adopted son of the former company president Han Bugyeom, born of his Korean-Russian ex-girlfriend? That's why, as the illegitimate child, he'd had such a bad relationship with his siblings. There were other rumors, too, that he'd had some genetic disorder, and that his wife, Jung Somi, used his adoptive father's frozen sperm to conceive their son, Han Suhyun. You can see why he'd be the modern-day Hong Gildong. And this woman, whoever she was, had been close enough to him to use Mr. Gildong as an acceptable nickname.

"I suddenly had a strange feeling. It had already crossed my mind that these might be President Han Junghyuk's memories. I'd already assumed they belonged to someone important, or else why would they have been preserved so carefully? And the only person of note who'd died recently in Patusan had been him. But the idea that President Han had felt this much love for someone, that seemed very odd to me. Not to mention that the feelings had to have been fairly recent, because the memory of love wanes over time.

"I started to feel jealous of Han Junghyuk. Of this love for a woman whose face or name I didn't know. I was jealous of his power and the things he could achieve with that power.

But more than anything else, I was jealous of his old-fashioned nickname, Mr. Gildong. So jealous that I lost the will, for a while, to track the woman down.

"Then, just five days later, I discovered her identity. It was inevitable, whether I was motivated or not—that's how close by she was all that time.

"It was a Sunday. I'd rushed through lunch in the cafeteria and was on my way to a souvenir store to buy a gift for my sister. The company newsfeed was playing on a large screen in the lobby. Some story about the parts for the African Space Consortium asteroid exploration craft that LK had recently launched. Just a bunch of faces I'd never seen mouthing things silently on the screen. At the very end, a woman appeared, to wrap things up, and this is where I froze in my tracks. It was her—it was her face. She couldn't be anyone else. Staring at her there on the screen, I was flooded with memories, a deluge so instantaneous that it brought on a splitting migraine.

"The news story ended and her face disappeared. I didn't bother searching for her name. I knew her name as surely as I knew her face. I had known of her even before I'd joined this company. It's just that I'd never been interested in her before.

"She was Kim Jaein. Head of the LK Space Development Research Center."

(PROBABLY) THE ONE THAT I LOVE

My face, so stern and attentive until now, almost caves in on itself as I try not to break into laughter. I could understand why someone would fall in love with Kim Jaein. Even if that someone were Han Junghyuk, well, distasteful as it was, I could still understand it. But this plot twist, with its introduction of Kim Jaein's familiar face, suddenly made the story feel thin, even clichéd.

Kim Jaein is the daughter of Han Sahyun, who was the only daughter of Han Bugyeom. Just like Han Junghyuk, Kim Jaein wasn't part of the family by blood. Han Sahyun had been a rebel, and with her parents' divorce, she'd become a militant anti-capitalist. She went on to publish three books—books that would incite the hatred of everyone associated with LK, and especially the Han family. Even more infuriating, all three volumes would become bestsellers, and the one novel among them—a thinly veiled autobiographical account—was even made into a seven-season television drama. Half of what people think about LK comes from these books. At the age of twenty-six, she married the actor Kim Lena, and Kim Jaein was born the next year. Han Sahyun had no interest in perpetuating her family's genetic line, and indeed Kim Jaein did not receive any of her genes. Han Bugyeom died when Han Sahyun was thirty-five, and if Sahyun herself hadn't been standing within the blast radius of the bomb that exploded during his funeral, she would certainly have found a place for the incident in her fourth book, cackling all the while as she wrote.

Han Sahyun had proclaimed that she would never take a cent of the Han family money, but Kim Lena was a much more prudent person. Kim Jaein was surreptitiously slipped into the main family so she would grow up with every advantage possible. Declining to compete for the throne of LK against her cousins, Kim Jaein became an astronomer. At nineteen, she coauthored a paper on a new method for detecting alien ecosystems that could sustain life. And by the time she was twenty-five, an exoplanet with a living ecosystem was found using her method. At thirty, as everyone expected, she was named director of the LK Space Development Research Center.

With a mother who was considered the most beautiful woman in the Korean-speaking world—and a biological father, if indeed there was one at all, who was obviously not ugly enough to compromise her phenotypic legacy—Kim Jaein was a magnet for others' eyes. She hated being put on public display, but photos and videos of her were always making the rounds on the Internet and in the media. The fanfics about her tailed off a little when she married the Korean-German test pilot Anton Choi, but they exploded again eight months after their wedding when he died in a skyhook accident.

That was simply who Kim Jaein was fated to be. Someone whose personal life was nothing special, but whose every possible path had been played out to exhaustion in fanfic. A person who, no matter which direction she chose, could only become a cliché. I'd never dreamed there might be a fanfic of her and Han Junghyuk together, but it wouldn't be so surprising if one existed—it takes all sorts to make the world go round, as they say. She would have been fourteen, already preparing to enter college, when the LK Group bought out Odyssey Incorporated and changed its name to LK Space. A fanfic where the space elevator was built just for Kim Jaein, that wouldn't be so odd. But one where President Han was the star of some romance? Creepy beyond imagining. Then again, the people who come up with these stories have been known to do much worse.

And, well, maybe they were right all along.

I take a moment to think about what I know regarding Kim Jaein. During the twelve years I've worked at LK, I've met her maybe about thirty times. Mostly when President Han was alive. Only three or four times did she come up in our conversations. Never anything personal. And I'd certainly never heard her call President Han "Mr. Gildong." If I had, I would've remembered. Because I can't think of anything further from President Han's character.

The Kim Jaein I know is dry, cold, businesslike, without a shred of human charm. Someone so charmless, in fact, that the beauty she inherited from her mother is actually intensified in comparison. The astronomers and aerospace engineers might see her differently, but that's the Kim Jaein I know. Sure, I get the worshipping-her-from-afar thing, I could do that, but I highly doubt it would be possible from up close. I still don't understand what it was about her that Anton Choi found so enthralling. He was an uncontainable, sexy beast of a man, completely unsuited for the likes of Kim Jaein, a figure as flat as a fashion magazine cutout.

I try to see it from President Han's perspective. They were, after all, both outsiders in the House of Han—maybe it was enough for him to feel an affinity toward her, although she was young enough to be his niece. Which could then have developed into love. Han Junghyuk had certainly been a Kim Lena fan. The physical similarity between mother and daughter might have stimulated his romantic imagination. There must be all sorts of factors I haven't considered until this moment. How much do I know about this man's heart, anyway? The Han Junghyuk I thought I knew is merely a figure of my imagination, pieced together according to my own wishes and needs, a few superficial puzzle pieces, nothing more. And Kim Jaein is no different. Who knows what's beneath that persona I'd seen as bland and tedious?

Choi Gangwu has stopped talking. I look at his face: unshaven, for at least a few days. The whiskers protruding from his cheeks are comical. I've described him as looking old for his years, but his expression right now is more like that of a puppy, a puppy that's had a rough go of it. And that face reminds me of someone—finally, I see it. Anton Choi! He looks vaguely like Anton Choi. And so do all the other candidates who were on those con artists' list. Low-rent versions of Anton Choi. Mechanically selected for their most superficial physical similarity to the real deal, completely ignoring the original's effortless sex appeal.

I think about President Han's appearance. A misshapen head, decked with bumps, small eyes that drooped at the corners, a mouth that seemed to curve in a perpetual smile—all of which made him look, in the end, like a clown. A small, thick lump of a body. Next to his siblings—inheritors of generations of genetic refinements introduced into the family by the women who married into it—his looks stood out even more. An ugly but commanding face, and because he'd used it to such great advantage while alive, it never occurred to me that he might be clinging to some resentment about his appearance. But that was before I learned he harbored a love for a woman decades younger than himself. I wonder if it disgusted him, to think of a body like his tangled up with someone like Kim Jaein.

A fragment of the dead president's mind, or something like it, had been inserted into the brain of a man who looked vaguely like her dead husband. And that man is now passionately in love with both Kim Jaein and the space elevator.

I've said before that preserving President Han's personal information would be a meaningless endeavor. I should've known there'd be one exception. The one thing Han Junghyuk would want to leave behind in death, that he'd want to survive him, to live forever. The thing I'd been too caught up in my own image of the late president to see.

Love.

WHAT WE DO NEHT

"What are you going to do now?" I ask.

"I don't know."

"Won't the biobot tell you what to do?"

"No."

"So you're just going to keep obsessing over the space elevator and Kim Jaein?"

He's convinced that I'm mocking him, and his face falls.

I get up from my chair. The air conditioner whines in the corner of the shipping container, hitting me with its breeze as I pace.

"Clearly this isn't some secret that only *we* are privy to. Someone, somewhere knows at least a part of what we know. AI or human, who knows, but all the puppet strings must lead back to a single point. The con artists rehired by LK Robotics probably know that the biobot they put into your brain was not ordinary, because you're the only one who got the royal treatment while everyone else got caught. Whoever it was that hired the man you know as Sekewael, they probably know something, too. Only they thought, wrongly, that what they were looking for was inside your Worm. And now we're running out of time, thanks to your recent incident, because more people will hold you suspect. Everyone is going to put their clues together and write their own narratives, which are bound to converge into one story."

After making a complete loop inside the container, I stand in front of Choi Gangwu and prod his forehead with my forefinger.

"Everyone wants what's inside Choi Gangwu's head. Preferably with you alive, but no matter if you die. They've got great equipment for that sort of recovery these days."

It's almost satisfying to watch his face turn pale.

I continue: "And what am I supposed to do now? I'm just some loose cog that's been rolling around in the LK system, making do with what I have. I'm stateless and my identity is faked. The old President Han had provided a protective fence around me for the past decade. I'm surviving but there's no way of knowing how long I'm going to last. What happens if Han Suhyun ousts Ross Lee and takes control of LK? He hates everything that has anything to do with his father. Not that he considers Han Junghyuk to be his father. Because his real father is the late Han Bugyeom, former president of LK, the man he calls his grandfather. Yes, those rumors are true. Han Bugyeom sired his biological grandson when the old man was informed of a genetic defect in his adopted son, Han Junghyuk. And Han Suhyun knows. Which means once Ross Lee is gone, it's the end of the line for me. Han Suhyun will scrub away every trace of Han Junghyuk, and I'll be top of his list. Hey, do you know what my real name is? Say it out loud. Don't think about it, just say it."

Stuttering a little, Choi Gangwu says my real name. The name I hadn't heard uttered by a single soul for the past twelve years.

"Search that name on the Internet and you'll get a sense of

my situation right away. Or don't, maybe those facts are already lurking in your mind. Han Junghyuk made a point of finding flawed people whom he could manipulate into absolute loyalty. But the problem for us is that after he died, there was no one who could protect us. Which means you're a second chance for me. To retire to someplace like Alaska, watch polar bears frolic from my peaceful deathbed."

"But I don't know anything."

"You don't know what you know or don't know. Your brain is a mess right now. We don't know how the Worm implanted by the company even connects with your brain at this point. And extracting it from you won't change the fact that your brain is a mess. You're wrapped up in delusions of grandeur and a fracturing personality because a dead man's ghost is inside your brain. You're even in love with a woman you've never met. You think you know all about the space elevator, but how do you know that knowledge is accurate? It belonged to someone else, it was only installed in your brain. And there could be a booby trap installed right along with it. The second we trigger it, your Worm might explode like O'Shaughnessy's. Or there could be a simple glitch—memory transfer is not a perfect technology. How much of your memory have you verified?"

A lot, apparently, judging from his suddenly confident expression. But I don't give him a chance to open his mouth.

"Do you know what I think? You have no thoughts and no plans. You want to go back to chasing butterflies and wallowing in your unrequited crushes on the space elevator and Kim Jaein. All the other young workers in this company throw themselves into maniacal self-improvement, but you? Never. Sure, to other people you look like you're trying to better yourself. But nothing you've done in your life goes beyond chugging down what others pour for you. And who cares? It's none of my business. But that lifestyle ended when O'Shaughnessy tried to pluck your Worm from your brain. It's open season on your ass now. Get as clever as a fox or die. Or maybe dying is a luxury in your case."

"Stop, please!"

"Would it make a difference if I do? You're lucky you met me. No, maybe it's not luck, maybe it's all part of the dead president's plan. Ross Lee is too dim to save his own life, and Han Suhyun's greed far outstrips his intelligence, which means all this could be some master plan put in place to save LK from their incompetence. Maybe it was President Han who hired O'Shaughnessy. As a way of telling us to get our act together. Or not—he was not one to have relied so heavily on luck. Or was he? What do I really know about him?"

My own frustration grinds me to a halt. Scratching my head, I manage to calm myself down and walk toward Choi Gangwu, who looks dazed.

"Try to be a little more selfish. That's the only way you—hell, even I—will ever survive. Take stock of every asset you possess and use them to the full. You could conquer LK if you play this right. Roll in the hay with Kim Jaein if you're lucky. You're living the fantasy of every tech nerd on the planet. But—"

"But I don't want to."

"And why not?"

"Roll in the hay, I mean. President Han never had such thoughts about Kim Jaein."

So the feelings the old man had for her were just familial affection? I guess that's possible. Because it's disgusting to be lovey-dovey about your niece, even if she's not technically your blood relation. And it wouldn't fit with what Choi Gangwu said about the old man's memories. Anyway, the details can be parsed out later.

"One thing at a time. The first thing we need to do right now is protect ourselves. Which means, the Worms inside our heads are the biggest problem. The company can keep an eye on us through our Worms. We don't know how your Worm and your brain are connected, which makes it tricky. But you'll be glad to know I have a friend who can help us. The problem is—"

"Is what?"

"Can we trust her?"

UNDER THE FAIRY'S WING

"A handsome devil."

"Don't say that in front of him. He'll think you're being serious."

"But I'm not sure if he really resembles Anton Choi."

"That's because some machine picked him out of a lineup. A person's superficial looks are such a small part of their overall charm."

"Oh yeah? Was there some other aspect to Anton Choi's so-called charm? I know *you* thought he was pretty. But aside from paying the price for pushing a spacecraft beyond its limit doing some fancy flight maneuvers, what *was* there to him? And who has a job as a test pilot in this day and age? You might as well sign up to be a lab rat." Sumac Graaskamp sighs, irritated. "Compared to him, it's Kim Jaein, whom you so readily dismiss as boring, who's the real deal. Discovering new biospheres in alien star systems, responsible for realizing half of the truly visionary goals at LK Space. It's not Han Suhyun, that mannequin grandchild of the former CEO, who's responsible for LK Space today, that's for sure. You might think the dead president's love for Kim Jaein is ridiculous, but it's not completely detached from reality, by any means."

"Uh, excuse me."

We turn to Choi Gangwu at his interruption, waiting for him to continue, but he doesn't. That was it. He just wanted to let us know he was still there, while we went on talking about him.

Graaskamp turns back to me and says, "So what's the plan?"

"Revitalize the information from the biobot and protect it from the company. That's why we came here."

"And what, pray tell, makes you think we can do that here?"

"Because we went through Neberu O'Shaughnessy's brain before we handed it back to you. We hadn't thought of the possibility of biobots then, only the Worm. But you know how it goes, when a little piece of new information opens your eyes to something you hadn't picked up on before. Which is how I now know that Green Fairy possesses quite a significant amount of technological know-how on biobots. Through some LK leak, evidently."

Graaskamp throws her head back in laughter. "What leak! Mac, it was LK Robotics that gave us the technology. They needed a means of testing it out on humans before going commercial. We were there *first*. This guy here came after."

"O'Shaughnessy was being manipulated by a biobot?"

"We suspected that might happen. So we brought in the four employees of ours who'd had the procedure and stuck another Worm into each of them. We can take care of this fellow as well if you like. The question is, of course, can you trust us?"

"Of course I can't. And it's extremely possible that you're lying to me because you want to filch his brain and sell it to the highest bidder. And there's also the chance that O'Shaughnessy went haywire under your control. But our likelihood of survival is still the highest in the scenario in which we trust you."

"Can't you ask Kim Jaein to protect you? If I were you, I'd trust her more than I'd trust me."

"I will. But before I do that, I need to know exactly what it is we have here."

"So you're saying the health and safety of your friend would be lovely and all, but you're going to suck as much meat out of the crab claws as humanly possible?"

"Is that so wrong?"

"No, but what does your cute friend think about that?"

I follow the line of Graaskamp's emaciated finger pointing to Choi Gangwu's stricken face. His emotions are completely exposed. I can almost make out the words in his brain just by looking at him. Sure, it's scary to have the whole world intent on plucking out your brain. But going to Kim Jaein and asking for help without anything to offer her, that wouldn't do for him, either, as a matter of pride. He wants to be a manly man and stand tall and equal before the woman he loves.

"Whatever it is, do it to me quickly," he squeaks.

"Well, dear, if that's what you really want. But don't forget this old queen here is trying to use your puppy-dog love to get what *he* wants," she says as she wags her finger at me.

The window, which until that moment had looked out onto a street full of little round cars and Haussmann-style buildings, completely blacks out. We've been duped—the office we'd thought was on the first floor of their building was actually somewhere underground. Green Fairy had been blocking our exit the entire time. But this situation reassures me more than anything. Graaskamp being so suspicious of us means this wasn't a trap of their making to begin with.

The door opens and four women bring in a gurney. The woman with the distractingly unkempt hair and wearing a white medical gown is Dr. Billabong Fang, if memory serves; we tried to hire her for External Affairs, but obviously she ended up at Green Fairy. Probably because she could be a little more illegal here.

The women force Choi Gangwu onto the gurney, six black-gloved arms pinning him down. Dr. Fang plops some steampunk mess of a helmet onto his head. As soon as it's in place, the four women leave by the door they entered.

"Is it really necessary to be in such a rush?" I ask.

"Has puttering around at LK dulled your sensibilities? If anything, we're already too late. You did manage to be fairly discreet coming here from Bandar Seri Begawan, I'll grant you that. But you can't just let your guard down because you made it inside Green Fairy. Our company is full of double agents, did you ever stop to think about that?"

"I figured you'd already be on top of that and get rid of them."

"Get rid of them? Why on Earth would I do that? When they're so delightfully useful."

WAR OF THE INVISIBLE BEASTS

The women haul Choi Gangwu to a parking lot where three trailer trucks are waiting. Choi Gangwu is loaded into one and Graaskamp and I get in another. The door closes and I can feel us picking up speed, but there is zero vibration. A moving laboratory, built by Green Fairy using the latest in Hollywood technology. A pair of "filming" spaceships, using similar technology, had gone up the space elevator a month before. To shoot some space-war reality show being produced in the Moon's orbit.

"Give me the keys to his Worm," says Graaskamp.

"Not until you explain to me what you're about to do."

"Fine. I'll keep it simple. By bringing Choi Gangwu here you effectively exposed him to all our mutual acquaintances. To whom he's been exposed, and who exactly is after him, we don't yet know. And we won't know until the double agents, whom we keep around for this very purpose, do their thing. These moving laboratories are the only alternative. We just finished remodeling our building, we can't be conducting business like this in there. No time to implant a new Worm, either. So we've got to use the LK Worm in his brain. Fortunately, we know a lot about the LK Worm through our own experiments. Those cheaters who got caught? We nabbed three of them off the street and brought them into our company and experimented on them. Don't make that face, they're fine. One of them has a bit of a memory issue, but we gave him an artificial hippocampus. He'll improve eventually. Maybe a chunk missing here and there, but who really wants to remember their teen years anyway? The brain parts modified by the biobot and by the Worm are basically the same, both are connected to the hippocampus. Using the basic function of the Worm to revitalize the remainder of the memories isn't that difficult. Well, for *us* it isn't, I don't know about the patient. If we break anything in there, I promise we'll do our very best to try to fix it. Anyway, the key?"

I take out my phone and send the key to her. As she scrolls through her own phone, a wall of the lab lights up—it's a screen, apparently—showing the inside of the lab Choi Gangwu is in. It's as if our two spaces are separated by a giant one-way mirror. Fang, having received the key code from Graaskamp, pulls a giant iron lever that looks like it's been repurposed from Dr. Frankenstein's lab. Choi Gangwu shudders and screams, and Dr. Fang laughs maniacally. I'm a little worried that she's enjoying herself so much—it makes me think Choi Gangwu's safety and well-being are rather low on her list of priorities.

There still isn't any vibration, but I do feel a sharp turn. I try through my Worm and phone to determine where we are, but they've both lost their signals; the trailer's shields are blocking transmission. The only information I'm privy to is feelings of speeding up and turning. Useful information normally, but Vientiane is such an unfamiliar city that I don't even know how to pronounce its name, much less its geography. I do see that the moving lab where Choi Gangwu is shown fidgeting on the screen is taking a different route from ours, because while we streak off in a straight line the other trailer is making a series of sharp right turns.

"We've been busy ourselves," Graaskamp says conversationally, "dissecting O'Shaughnessy's brain down to the cellular level and looking into every bit of backup data uploaded from his Worm. The biobot was a Trojan horse, it had secretly manipulated our company Worm within his brain. And were we completely in the dark about that? No, we knew. We figured it was a way into the internal workings of LK. I lied to you that time on Pala, sorry. Well—not really.

"When O'Shaughnessy started acting strange, we picked up on it quickly. O'Shaughnessy himself had an idea that he was being controlled, and the controller also knew that we knew. It was all a game of who was how many steps ahead, and we lost. Those bastards were clever—turns out the four who looked untouched had also had their Worms secretly manipulated, throwing us off track when we were analyzing O'Shaughnessy's Worm data. Even when we thought we'd accounted for that already . . . Well, you know how it is. No such thing as a surprising twist in these chaotic times; we're not living in an Agatha Christie novel.

"But at least we knew whom we were dealing with: LK's notorious Security. Or some organization within Security. Every trail leads back to there. We were about eighty percent sure before O'Shaughnessy died, and now we're ninety-six percent sure. Watching External Affairs stumble around like you all have two left feet made me even more certain, because if there's one LK division External Affairs is in the dark about, it's Security. Right? Like mitochondria in a cell, you were all your own companies before being absorbed into the cytoplasm of LK, and you're still competing with each other. There's no such thing as cooperation between the strata of your corporation.

"Of course, this isn't all up to Security. There's someone above them as well. And if that someone is Kim Jaein, you're both walking into the lion's den."

"I don't think it's her. She has no motive."

"Are you sure? And do you even know what motives the others had? How well do you know what's going on at LK's Mount Olympus? You're assuming, so far, that the important information was grafted into this simpleton's brain and the LK Worm is clean, but I don't think so. There's a second program in the Worm, one that can easily pass through External Affairs screening. It's been absorbing and analyzing the contents of your friend's brain all this time. It might've sent it on to somewhere else, but we don't know where that is yet. Extracting that Worm from O'Shaughnessy was not as useless an endeavor as you think."

"Why would Security go through all that trouble? No one cared about Choi Gangwu until then. All they had to do was send a couple of specialists to his apartment at night and switch out his Worm. No need for all this fuss and murder. Or the sheer bother of manipulating some employee in a private spy agency."

"But that happened regardless. The puppeteer had a plan in which doing so made sense. We just don't know what that plan is yet. So what I'm saying is—"

Graaskamp suddenly falls silent and brings a finger to her lips. The lab swerves to the side and so do we. I look at the screen: Choi Gangwu continues to scream in the lab, which is now running on a straight track. Had it ever stopped? I've been too deep in my conversation with the Green Witch to remember Choi Gangwu existed.

The screams abate. The helmet comes off and so do the restraints. The four women push Choi Gangwu's unconscious body from the chair and onto an object that looks like an inflatable child's high chair. The screen, along with the wall, rips open and the lab shakes—the Hollywood machine that keeps things stable inside has been damaged. Dr. Fang shouts something into the camera and the screen on our side goes black.

Graaskamp flicks a finger, and a long, dolphin-like two-seater motorcycle hanging on the wall across from the screen unfolds itself as it descends. Its wheels slide out before it reaches the floor, and the bike flickers before turning almost invisible. Following Graaskamp's orders, I take a seat behind her, where I am soon enclosed by a canopy that reaches up from the back and clamps down around me.

"I suggest you grab onto something."

The back of the laboratory opens and we go flying out.

The truck that had been towing our trailer lab is lying on its side in the middle of a gigantic junkyard. Every surface is pockmarked and torn from the attack we'd sustained. Flying drones and robot cars in various states of destruction are rolling around it. A drone with a flickering invisibility membrane that had engaged in battle just a moment ago soars off toward the west. Half of the drones are on our side, the other half, who knows? A drone with a malfunctioning invisibility membrane is falling in the distance; it's impossible to tell whose side it's on.

My Worm activates a window: it's a map. The red dot running westward is the motorcycle we are riding. From farther west, a green dot speeds toward us, surrounded by yellow dots in hot pursuit. Which are in turn surrounded by blue dots.

Another window. It's a fisheye-lens view of Dr. Fang, spittle flying as she's shouting something, but in a language I can't discern, not Pashto or Laotian or . . . Is it pig Latin? It may well be.

A third window. Camera footage taken from one of our drones. The just barely discernible outlines of a motorcycle with an invisibility membrane. It's running through the junk-yard, surrounded by blinking drones shooting needles at it. From far away there's another bike running toward it, along with the drones that had departed the trailer lab with us. I turn off all the windows and see the almost invisible bike running straight toward us. The shots and explosions all around make reality itself appear to shatter—I grit my teeth and close my eyes. I'm too old to be caught up in this.

The bike turns and jumps. Two machine-gun barrels pro-truding from the front fire needle bombs into the air, and two drones fall to the ground, making little earthquakes upon im-pact. I open one eye and give a shout: two drones, their invis-ibility membranes disabled, are flying toward the other bike. One of them collides into a third drone and crashes to the side, but the remaining drone kamikazes directly into the bike. Yel-low flames, shrapnel everywhere.

The sky flashes for a moment, and my Worm goes offline; almost simultaneously, all the drones shooting needles at each other lose their invisibility and crash. A drone had set off its EMP bomb.

I leap off the bike. The other bike is twisted beyond recog-nition. Where are the bodies of Choi Gangwu and Dr. Fang? There's half a body lying under a bit of debris, which I lift out of the way.

A mannequin. Wearing a rubber mask made to look like Dr. Fang.

There's cackling behind me. And I realize, at once, that I'm part of a game the Green Witch has been playing all along.

"So," I finally say, "what part of all that was real?"

"Nothing you saw on that screen was real, Mac. So, what do you think? Pretty realistic, am I right? A little melodramatic, but there's no fun in relentless realism."

"What about the truck Choi Gangwu was on?"

"All three trucks were red herrings. We wouldn't conduct such an important operation on a truck, for the love of god. Your friend hasn't left our building this entire time. Actually, no. His operation ended ten minutes ago and we sent him outside."

A NAME REMEMBERED TOO LATE

My Worm comes back online. It's empty. My personal assistant program with the voice of George Sanders is gone, as is everything else that isn't the basic operating system. I try to connect with the LK mainframe but no dice. I've now been completely separated from the herd. How am I to explain this to them? I try telling myself that I'll think up an excuse later, but I can't shake my feeling of queasiness.

The very minimum of safeguards are in place, of course. I'd given myself a five-day vacation when I left for Bandar Seri Begawan. The optics aren't too bad; sure, there was a recent murder attempt, but Miriam is already on it with her usual type-A personality, rendering my presence redundant. Choi Gangwu and I had taken different planes to Patusan, but to anyone checking in on the operations of External Affairs, it will all look like precautions I'm taking to prevent another attempt on Choi Gangwu's life. A double layer of convincing lies. I'd activated my avatar in case of an emergency; it'll do as a scarecrow unless some truly tricky situation ensues. Even if the avatar is unmasked, there's a contingency plan, and one after that as well. That's my job: lying and wriggling my way out of things.

The problem is how this wriggling will look to Rex Tamaki. Tamaki and I, from the moment we met, have been playing a kind of chess match with each other. On paper, our job descriptions shouldn't give either of us cause for wariness over who gets to handle what. But the natural order of things, when a company brings two different criminal organizations into its fold, is for those organizations to be wary of each other. Especially when the boss who hired them suddenly dies, depriving them of their mutual cause for allegiance. The dead president enjoyed the tension between our two divisions and created synergy from it, but his somewhat less perverse successors were probably thinking it would be more efficient to can one of us, or else fuse us into one division. The only reason the status quo has continued is that Ross Lee, in his bumbling, hesitant laziness, hasn't gotten around to reorganizing us.

Security will always have the upper hand when it comes to intel, which is why External Affairs will always be at a disadvantage. That's why we've been more vigilant with our recon efforts than they have with theirs. What they do in the name of the company's security normally has nothing to do with us. Unless the target of their conspiracy is External Affairs itself.

There's only one thing I'm sure of when it comes to Rex Tamaki: he has no beliefs, vision, or political convictions. He is the most profane and superficial person I know. Every chance he gets he's after one woman or another. And he craves adrenaline. Yet another reason we're disadvantaged in this game. Unlike me, Rex enjoys playing it. He's had plenty of time to uncover my true identity—the only reason he hasn't played that card yet, even after the death of the company president, is that he loves having it up his sleeve. The world is a playground to him, and External Affairs just another toy. It's also why Security falls just short of fully cooperating with Han Suhyun.

Because to Tamaki, Han Suhyun is the most boring person in the world.

I don't think Security is behind the attempted murder of Choi Gangwu. It was too crudely executed, for one thing. And I can't think of any reason they would do it crudely on purpose. It's more likely they're running around looking for the real culprit, just like we are. But how close have they gotten? And if they've solved the mystery already, how are they going to use it?

I've got to trust Miriam for now. Because no one is more sensitive to Security's dealings than she is.

I get up and look in the mirror. A face that's similar to the one I had before my plastic surgery, but ten years younger. Hair dyed dark brown and cut short. The transplant feels a little odd but nothing intolerable. It took only two hours. This makes me wonder what other tricks Green Fairy's disguise team has in their arsenal. I decide not to think about the inevitable side effects for now.

I open the door and leave the room. Following a long corridor, I come upon a lounge. Two patients are playing Ping-Pong while another two stare blankly at a screen: on it, an orchestra made up entirely of women wearing white dresses is playing a twentieth-century waltz.

I sit down on a sofa and log on to the hospital's public records using my Worm. A man with an unfamiliar name but with my current face has been an inpatient here for the past four days. The man's CV is also quite convincing. As long as no one tries to get me to talk in Tagalog, I think I can get away with pretending to be him. I can't find anyone who might be Choi Gangwu. Maybe he's hidden even more deeply.

Sumac Graaskamp enters the lounge, accompanied by a

doctor. I get up from the sofa and casually walk over to them. The doctor splits off and heads into a nearby ward. Graaskamp and I get on an elevator. We'd been on the second floor; the elevator takes us to the twelfth.

Choi Gangwu is in room 1205. He still hasn't regained consciousness. His face is swollen, stuffed with augmentations by the Green Fairy doctors. They haven't been activated, so he still looks more or less like himself. Except clean shaven, probably for the surgery.

"We've collected the drones that attacked us and have found out who tried to kill us," said Graaskamp. "Well, it's more of a what than a who. TGGA Logistics and HYO Services."

"What's all that?"

"The letters don't stand for anything. They were probably selected at random. Both companies were created by AI that emerged organically from global networks. It's something that's been happening for the past three years. It started in Laos. And there are a few more such companies in Kenya and Rwanda, but I bet that's not all. Everyone is kind of letting it happen, curious to see what comes of it. It's good to be prepared, I think. The sun is setting on humanity. Your LK will inevitably turn into an AI persona of its own someday.

"There's no trace of Security. Everything seems to have been wiped during the drones' attack. But the Laotian government had put them under surveillance, so we've got some data. They don't want to share intel with us, but we've got traces of traces. And the cops are moving on the evidence of those traces."

"You don't think it's bait meant for Green Fairy?"

"We've prepared for that possibility, but why would they do such a thing? It'll just waste everyone's time, including theirs. Choi Gangwu's brain has been more or less cleaned up, his

Worm backed up. But we can't read his Worm data, unfortunately. We need his brain for that. So let me know when he wakes up."

The Green Witch exits, and I am left alone with Choi Gangwu. I stare at his body lying motionless on the bed and groan as I pull up a chair. It's like being left alone with a dog I'd just rescued. Like I'd done a stupid good deed and now the consequences are snowballing. Was this the best thing I could've done under the circumstances? Wouldn't it have been better to secure what treasures the former president had given me and leave LK, go into hiding? I guess it's not too late now. If I choose to stay with Green Fairy, they'll give me something to do, at least. Surely Han Suhyun has no earthly reason to bother with little old me anymore if I just disappear?

The problem is, he has many earthly reasons. Up until recently, I had made a huge fuss about how important I was, all in the name of trying to protect myself after the president's death, implying that he had given me more than he actually had. It was also an attempt to boost my division and win against the other divisions in the company. But now that I think back on it, I was an idiot. Han Suhyun is an idiot, too, but at least he's not alone. He's surrounded by cunning players who have filled their pockets by always having his back. They're a bit scattered at the moment, but it's only a matter of time before they regroup under him. Who knows how this will manifest once Ross Lee leaves the company. Tamaki will probably choose which side he's on, at last. Seeing how little fun he'd be able to get out of me then, he'd leave me like a cat leaves a half-dead bird.

The only way I can survive now is to make all my fuss, my nonsense, come true.

Choi Gangwu squirms. The monitor lights up above his headboard and there's a chime. He opens his mouth and moans. He's squirming again, the whole metal bed is shaking. Then he grabs my left arm and starts cursing me out—harsh, but his words are in Korean and weirdly old-fashioned, almost archaic, making him seem more ridiculous than intimidating.

Two nurses run up to us and separate him from me, injecting his neck with a tranquilizer. The screams subside into sobs. I shoulder my way between the nurses; Choi Gangwu's eyes, unfocused, suddenly grow wide as he sees my face.

"I killed them, Mac! I killed those people!"

It's Choi Gangwu's voice, but something about his cadence reminds me of the former president.

"Killed who?"

"Adnan Ahmad. And all those people . . ."

The tranquilizer kicks in and his voice grows faint. I leave him to the nurses and walk out of the room, in a daze.

THE PEOPLE I KILLED

Adnan Ahmad was a geologist employed by LK Construction, the son of a fisherman on Patusan, where he grew up. He went to college in Taprobana and obtained his PhD at the Korea Advanced Institute of Science and Technology. LK Construction had sought him out from the start, thinking of how Patusan's Swiss cheese geological structure made it perfect for constructing underground cities. Somewhere on Patusan there's a plaque with his name on it, which also includes a three-line poem written by a company poet. This poet was hired by President Han to live for a year on Patusan and write scores of poems commemorating the deaths and disappearances of the construction workers of the city. I've heard it said the poems are quite good for something done on corporate commission, but I don't know enough about Korean poetry to have an opinion.

Adnan was a giant, almost two meters tall, with shoulder-length curly hair. He wasn't handsome but his shy smile made a good impression on others. Unlike the Koreans he worked with, he didn't laser off his beard, either. A clever and skillful man but also simple folk and honest. We dated for about a week and had sex twice. I'm not saying he was homosexual, necessarily. He was simply a young man who craved a variety of stimuli and experiences.

Ten years ago . . . Any Patusan person who had any kind of important decision-making power at LK would've had to make a difficult choice—even more difficult for someone as honest as Adnan. Do I become a good dog for a multinational corporation or do I fight for my people? Most of us, being what we are, would find some position in the middle. But that didn't do for Adnan. He was equally passionate about the space elevator and proud of his Patusan identity, and it was impossible for him to compromise between the two feelings.

This was before the Patusan Liberation Front came into being. Back then, in its nascent state, the Front was merely a mélange of aimless resentment, anger, and opinions. Adnan, amid all of that, tried to be true to everything he loved. It was a dangerous tightrope to walk.

Many people attempted to take advantage of Adnan. This innocent geologist tried to keep his head amid the chaos, acting only in accordance with his will. Naturally he was sought after by both sides, and all he ended up succeeding in was making lots of enemies. It was a truly disturbing turn of events. Adnan had never dreamed he'd become so political, that he'd be a target of hate for so many people.

President Han Junghyuk liked Adnan. He was peeved by him, yes, but he liked him. That little bastard doesn't look for the easy way out, he has a spine, he would say. Sometimes he'd call him an opportunist, a bat flitting from one side to the other, but the real opportunists were the people surrounding Adnan, political clarity being the easiest weapon for opportunists to deploy. In any case, the president was more than ready to kick Adnan to the curb the moment he got in the way of company profits.

Then the incident with the three lawyers happened.

The three men were Lee Jaechan, Kang Youngsu, and Jung Mungyeong, all part of the legal department at LK. We call them lawyers, but they were really certified con men, adept in the art of slithering their way through the decidedly non-space-agey, archaic maze that is the Patusan legal system. They had more work than you might think—it's astonishing what can happen in a Patusan courtroom.

If they'd just done their jobs, their names wouldn't be etched in my memory, but of course they had to go and do something unforgivable. One rainy Sunday evening, they crawled out of the new Patusan City into the old and raped two fourteen-year-old girls on their way home from visiting their friends. One of the girls was killed in the process.

This was a planned assault. Any workers with the Worm in their brains were very unlikely to be able to carry out a pre-meditated crime of this magnitude; the Worm, at the slightest sign of violence, would have alerted the company immediately. This means that they'd tampered with their Worms beforehand and were going to use the fact that they had Worm implants as a sort of alibi down the line. Which also implies that they'd stalked their victims for months before the deed.

Despite having been drugged, the surviving victim managed to remember the face of one of the perpetrators, and that there were two other people with him. But there was no DNA evidence to be found, and no one to contradict the trio's alibi. It was obvious they'd manipulated surveillance footage and drones to shore up their lies, but clear as it was that tampering had occurred, the evidence was circumstantial. Anti-LK sentiment, which had always been simmering in the background, suddenly boiled over. To make matters worse for the company, it was election season. The dead victim's mother had an important role in the Doran Party, and despite the native voters being in the absolute minority, they could still seriously thwart the growth of LK's operations on the island.

President Han Junghyuk had wanted a neat and clean solution. Rex Tamaki, a new arrival at Security at the time, took over the case. He requested a four-day vacation, flew to Jakarta alone, kidnapped the lawyers one by one, and brought them back to Patusan in crates.

The perpetrators emerged from their drug-induced comas in front of the surviving victim and the dead victim's mother. President Han explained to the girl and the mother that resolving this issue through legal channels of justice was bound to prove impossible, whereupon he presented them with seven pairs of different handsaws, each personally designed by Rex Tamaki to deliver the greatest amount of suffering. Tamaki politely explained which part of the human anatomy produced the most pain when a spinning sawtooth was applied. The Patusans each chose an instrument, and the rapists, after an hour and a half of wailing, finally gave up the ghost. Security cleaned up and removed the bodies, and an odd boat accident was reported in the ocean near Jakarta. Tamaki, compared to the lawyers, was even more of an expert at coming up with alibis.

A happy ending. But the three criminals were petty, even from beyond their watery grave. Enraged that the company was unwilling to protect them, they'd secretly stashed a horde of LK Space legal memos in a data locker. Once they went missing, the keys to this locker were automatically delivered to various political powers-that-be in Patusan society.

Most of the fallout was taken care of by the legal team, and the rest fell under the purview of External Affairs. This was precisely the job that LK had bought out our company for. We did our best to tie up the loose ends, but this leak exposed vari-

ous loopholes that had previously been buried under moun-
tains of case law, namely that a judge could now rule that native
Patusans were entitled to a 40 percent share of the land where
the new city was being built. Anti-LK sentiment, meanwhile,
was at an all-time high, no thanks to the brutal crimes, and it
wasn't about to settle down anytime soon. There was only so
much ground the mother of the dead victim could cover; she
had blood on her own hands and therefore could not publicly
credit Han Junghyuk for delivering justice. As far as the world
was concerned, it was fate that killed the rapists, not LK.

"But what does Adnan Ahmad have to do with all this?"
Graaskamp asks.

"He was one of the fifty people entitled to that forty percent
share and a cousin of the dead girl. And an absolutely essential
brain for that stage of LK's development on the island. Also,
as I mentioned, he was someone the president actually liked.
Adnan suddenly became the most important person in Patusan, and despite his natural reticence, he took up the cause,
bringing together all the Patusan employees at LK to pressure
management.

"President Han's great advantage was that he knew the
strengths and weaknesses of every opponent he ever faced. So
what were Adnan's strengths and weaknesses? His honesty—
the fact that he had nothing to hide. A simple, straightforward
man. He'd come off as a bit complex before, considering how
conflicted his loyalty to Patusan and his loyalty to the company
could appear from the outside. But even there he was simple.
The situation was complex, but *he* wasn't. That's why when he
made a move, even those who were against him would move
with him. There's a certain power that only simple and honest
people have.

"What to do in such a situation? The president had to take a gamble. He called Adnan in and told him how the rapists had died. By sharing this secret, he made Adnan an accomplice. I think Adnan felt he'd been dirtied. He must've agreed that justice had prevailed, but he could no longer be honest. I'm sure that's when the others sensed his change, that he was hiding something. They assumed he had accepted a favor from the president. Not that they were wrong, necessarily. This is how the president, in a very simple move, created fractures in the gang of fifty."

"How on Earth is this the first time I'm hearing of this? I realize I don't know everything about LK, but an incident of this magnitude?"

"Well, the whole thing ended with a whimper. At least from the outside. The company and the fifty came to a pretty easy compromise. Anti-LK sentiment was eventually tamped down by the Doran Party. And a public endorsement of LK from the dead child's mother didn't hurt. Adnan and a few of his compatriots died in a radical Christian terrorist bomb attack. People were generally sad and regretful about it. LK was inconvenienced, as no one knew the geological structure of this island better than Adnan and they had lost one of their most essential employees. He had that mysterious ten percent of knowledge that AI can't access yet. Something about such knowledge being possible to obtain only through experience? Not that I have any idea what that means.

"I believed this story, too. There was no reason not to. The people of Patusan have always clashed with LK. I didn't know anything about the execution of the rapists at the time, which is why I didn't realize how serious the problem had been. Nothing has changed much. I'm still in the dark on a lot of things. This ignorance is by design, all part of keeping our lies pure."

"Then what really happened, if not some Jesus freaks on a rampage?"

"Thirty-eight out of the fifty lost their lives. They'd charged into our construction site in protest, believing the company was using Adnan to manipulate them. I don't think they had intended for anything to happen, really, they probably just wanted to have it out with Adnan. And Adnan was trying to defend himself and the company. He must've told them about what had actually happened to the rapists. The truth might have worked in our favor, but the circumstances weren't right. They didn't care that the rapists were dead, but they realized the truth in this case could help them upend the ruling Doran Party and stage a new attack on the company. Security got involved, and President Han gave his approval. They were in such a dangerous spot geologically, the rock being filled with giant holes and all, that there probably wasn't much actual butchering of the Patusan protesters to stress them out. It had always been a precarious geological formation, the cave-in was kind of inevitable in a way. Even if the company hadn't lifted a finger.

"Everything in the official narrative from that point on is fiction. Thirty-three of the thirty-eight who perished were replaced with virtual personas by the company. These scarecrows who existed only on paper and on the Internet lived out the lives of the dead. Most of them had been part of the Patusan diaspora and were de facto foreigners on the island, so it was easy to pull off the ruse. But Adnan and his friends couldn't be replaced so easily. This is why we brought in the radical Christians. It wasn't a total fabrication, they did plant bombs in the main tower. Twice. And they got caught. But their organization is so decentralized that even many of their own members had no idea what was going on. Some of them still believe their organization really did the bombing."

"And the whole time External Affairs knew nothing?"

"We sensed that we didn't have the whole picture. Tamaki, you see, would walk around grinning all the time."

"But this makes no sense. It's just not very Han Junghyuk, if you know what I mean. I get that rapists walking about in broad daylight would annoy him, because he thought that would harm the company in some way. But there were so many other, safer ways to take care of this. If the rapists could manufacture evidence, so could Security. Even without that hassle, was there really no other way a giant company like LK could take care of three rogue lawyers? According to you, Han Junghyuk had a hundred different ways he could've solved this predicament, but he chose to act like Ernst Stavro Blofeld."

"Who?"

"Never mind who, this is what happens when you mess up the first time: things just spiral out of control. Didn't Han have any intelligent people or AI around him? Did he just ignore them? Why did such a clever realist act so stupidly?"

"He was in love."

"What? Are you having a stroke?"

"It's true. He was in love. The new Patusan City, the space elevator, these were gifts Han Junghyuk was giving to Kim Jaein. President Han didn't want anything to mar this gift. If there was a smear of rape, he had to wipe it away, quickly. He had to use a punitive system more perfect than jail to destroy the rapists' very existence. That's why his actions made sense to him at the time. But they were done in a context of personal desire that he could not share with anyone else, and that's what caused the incident to snowball. Which leads us to today, where all the guilt that he buried in himself is bubbling up to the surface in Choi Gangwu's brain."

MISSING

Choi Gangwu's hospital room is empty.

The bed is unmade and the wardrobe open. Every electronic device, including the lights, is turned off. In the garbage bin is a piece of crumpled paper with my name on it. He seems to have tried to leave me a message and given up.

"So how smart is your little friend?" asks Graaskamp.

"We're talking about a man whose greatest joy in life up until a few years ago was chasing butterflies."

"That doesn't answer my question. Is he smart enough to break through our security measures and escape the hospital?"

She looks insulted. How dare this imbecile compromise Green Fairy security! I need to placate her by proving he isn't as empty-headed as he looks.

"He knows everything about Patusan and the space elevator, thanks to biobots. But they wouldn't have helped him escape. This isn't something he could've done on his own—someone must have helped him. Once his Worm activated, it must have automatically logged on to the outside."

"So you're telling me a lepidopterist with grand delusions of being Han Junghyuk has broken out with the help of some mysterious person and is now wandering the streets of Vientiane?"

I try to calculate the possibility of the "ghost" of Han Junghyuk, stored somewhere as digital data, interfacing with Choi Gangwu's brain through the Worm. Using his new, young, healthy, and handsome body to entice Kim Jaein. A plausible scenario, but all the less likely for being so plausible. President Han didn't operate with such transparence. I also can't imagine Kim Jaein, a woman as frigid as a heroine in a nineteenth-century gothic novel, falling for such a conceit. The whole thing is just, well, completely distasteful, and President Han knew it; that's why he never revealed his feelings in life. But it doesn't become any less distasteful just because he changed his body.

The technological part is also a mystery. Copying and sending a part of one's memories isn't that difficult. But an entire consciousness? Grafted onto a living person's brain? It may be possible one day, but it isn't now. LK has all sorts of stupendous inventions hiding up its sleeve, but technology of that caliber could never have been kept a secret for so long, because all technology exists in a very fine web of interconnected knowledge.

Which means, the man who's on the run right now is still very much Choi Gangwu. A man who possesses some of Han Junghyuk's memories, who can pierce through Green Fairy security. But whose idea had it been to escape from the hospital? Whose free will?

Choi Gangwu's, of course. It's the kind of compulsive and simpleminded choice only he would make.

On my phone, I process the data handed over by the Green Fairy AI. There are some potential lines of movement. Choi Gangwu's measures to hide his tracks, effective for about twenty minutes, are beginning to lose their effectiveness. The

effort he went to is truly, disproportionately massive; he seems
to have brought a bulldozer when a trowel would've done the
job. All of Vientiane's traffic is in gridlock as a result.

Let's pretend I'm Choi Gangwu. If I were frightened and had
the power to freeze an entire city in its tracks, what mode of
transportation would I use? Not a passenger vessel. Something
faster and more flexible and private. Something that can take
me out of Vientiane as quickly as possible.

I search every mode of transport controlled by LK Vientiane. Nothing comes up that would do. But the fact that one of
the possible lines of movement touches the harbor does strike
me as meaningful.

Graaskamp and I leave the hospital on her dolphin motorcycle and race to the harbor. I use my External Affairs codes—
thank god they still work—and enter the company warehouse.
There's one thing on the manifest that's missing: an executive-
level four-person seaplane. Fortunately, there's another one
standing by.

"What are you going to do to your friend once you catch
him?" asks the Green Witch as she watches me force open the
lock mechanism on the cockpit.

"I'm going to be very reasonable and persuasive."

"And how would either of you know what's 'reasonable' in
this situation?"

I've got nothing to say to that.

SOMEONE ELSE'S SIN

I land the seaplane at Tamoé, where the other seaplane is parked in one of the harbors, right out in the open, as if to mock me. It's empty, obviously. When I approach, the plane seems to flinch like a living animal and moves slowly away before taking off on its own. Toward Patusan, I observe, not Laos. Once it arrives in Patusan, the warehouse robots will give it a cleaning and a recharge before it flies back to Vientiane on its own. Nothing I need to bother about.

With no plan in mind, I start walking toward the Gondal Quarter. I doubt Choi Gangwu will be on Tamoé. If President Han really did wake up in a corner of Choi Gangwu's brain, he wouldn't be wasting his time in some sad excuse for a city, he'd be at the largest garbage dump he'd made in his life as LK president—namely the Gondal Quarter.

The Tamoé government had done their best to eliminate Gondal, or at least make it habitable, but they'd failed. We live in an era where AI works its magic on municipal planning and administration, freeing the world of poverty, and yet there are still places where the technology comes up short. Garbage always accumulates somewhere. LK tried turning this place into an idealistically self-sufficient community, like they did with Pala's settlements, but the inhabitants here are different, they have no sense of purpose or determination to do anything. And everyone who was a better fit for Pala is already in Pala.

I come here maybe once or twice a year, but I know my way around well enough. Even without the Worm I can make my way through the stacks of rusting shipping containers. I know where certain persons of interest live, and meanwhile drones the size of flies are busy flitting around and sending data to External Affairs. I may have cloaked my landing and disguised myself using Green Fairy's facial augmentation technology, but my division will know I'm here soon enough.

I walk through the alleyways, ignoring the places Choi Gangwu would never go—that eliminates about 60 percent of the Quarter. What's left are the little safe houses Security has squirreled away here and there. And since he's here with no plan, Choi Gangwu will need a place to sit down and think. How many container safe houses are there anyway? I search on my phone: seven, total.

The first container on the list is being used as a storage space. The second has five squatters, children with dead-looking eyes, data-drug addicts by the look of it. The third container is on a hill. I hate inclines, but it's the fastest way up.

I hear whistling, in a three-part harmony. I turn around. Three teenage boys—who knows where they came from—are tailing me, whistling LK jingles. The different themes to the space elevator, LK, Patusan. They seem to have discovered that the chord progressions of the jingles are similar enough to whistle together in harmony. I sense faint hostility in their faces, but their emaciated frames and bloated stomachs reveal that they do not pose much of a threat. Why live like this, I wonder. Lend your brains and bodies for just five hours every day to LK and you'll be free from this hellhole full of rapists and thieves, getting all the food and medicine you need, instead of spending your life as a walking threat to society.

I reach the third trailer. I'm thinking of scaring them away with my gun, but the kids stop in their tracks and chew on some unidentifiable brown sticklike thing, watching me. I wipe the sweat off my brow and calm my breathing. Gnats fly into my face. No doubt half of these insects had been endangered before being revived by LK biologists.

The door is unlocked. All the windows are blacked out. I turn on the lamp function on my phone and step inside; there's something sticky covering the floor.

Blood. I'm standing right in a pool of it.

I see, in the middle of the pool, a large, pale hand. It's not Choi Gangwu's. Too big and too hairy.

The hand is connected to an arm as muscular as a wrestler's. That arm in turn has been sliced off from the shoulder. The torso from which it was removed still has a head attached to it, barely. I turn the head over with my foot. Large gray eyes, closely shorn blond hair, a carnotaurus tattoo covering half the forehead. Haakon Larsen. Rex Tamaki's right-hand man.

Beside Larsen lies the weapon that cut him into pieces. It looks like a hand-grip strengthener at first glance. But when I pick it up, I feel a tug: another hand-grip strengthener jumps out of the dark, the two parts connected by an LK tube. A part they mass-produce on Patusan. It looks simple, the weapon, but I know it's strong enough to slice through a grown man like he's butter. I can see it now: a mere gun would never satisfy the sadistic urges of someone like Larsen, which is why he brought this corpse slicer to throw around. I guess that didn't work out. He's the kind of man who has approximately sixty nunchucks on display in his home. I knew he'd die like this someday.

I look around for any of Choi Gangwu's body parts. Nothing. But there does seem to be a ripped, bloody jacket—it's Choi Gangwu's. There's also a bit of underwear, seemingly Larsen's, torn to be used as a bandage. Choi Gangwu must not be injured too badly, then.

I come out of the shipping container. The children are still chewing their sticks, watching me. They probably saw Choi Gangwu and Haakon Larsen enter this container. I don't sense curiosity in their gazes. We're not that interesting to them.

I look at the village down the hill. LK's Security Division had made a mess in one of the plazas. There's bright lighting there, and people are gathered. Something draws me to it, and I make my way down.

An old woman is giving a speech. I don't understand it. Buginese, probably, a language I'd never even thought to learn. If my Worm were connected to the company I would have interpreter support, but as it is I'm just standing among the crowd, listening to an alien tongue.

Suddenly, the crowd moves. I hear, also, a familiar voice: Choi Gangwu. He's walking up to the stage, wearing a shirt soaked in blood. And speaking Buginese. I can tell he's reading from a transliterated script that his Worm is beaming into his brain, stuttering his way through it. I can't understand what he's saying, but the names he mentions are all too familiar. Names I'd refreshed in my memory very recently. The names of the thirty-eight who had been murdered. I don't need a translation to understand the short sentences that follow. *I killed these people. I'm a murderer.* He's trying to atone for the sins he's inherited. I recall the statue of Mary in his room. Is this Catholic psychology? And isn't it also suicide?

The audience comes out of their stupor and they rush the stage. They drag Choi Gangwu away. I can't see anything, but

I hear screaming, loud and clear. Unholstering my gun, I walk toward the screams.

Gunshots come from behind me. The crowd falls silent. I turn around and see someone I'd never have dreamed would be here: Mayor Nia Abbas. She's flanked by four women carrying guns. The crowd parts like the Red Sea, revealing the bloody body of Choi Gangwu on the ground.

The mayor speaks in Buginese to the crowd. Yet again I'm in the dark, but her manner of speaking is, as always, matter-of-fact, relaxed, as if nothing out of the ordinary is taking place. A few people shout, but the mayor shrugs and answers in a steady tone. The crowd loses steam and begins to scatter.

Choi Gangwu struggles to his feet. His dirty face is locked in a grimace, no doubt because the mayor has just turned his dramatic martyring into a public nuisance.

"Did you ever stop to think about the people who would have to clean up after you? Sure, it would be all over for *you* once you're dead but what happens to *us*, we who've run this investigation for years? And what about that crowd, the people you were so willing to turn into murderers for your convenience?"

"B-but—"

"You LK people need to start living in the present," the mayor persists. "It's not enough that you've been aping the actions of nineteenth-century imperialists, now you're aping their guilt as well. Can't you afford to skip a few steps? What the hell were you thinking, in this the age when we're taking elevators into space? Do we look like savages in a Victorian novel to you?"

SECOND CHECK

"Tamaki did do a good job," admits the mayor. "We didn't know about the scarecrows replacing the cave-in victims at first, either. And neither did External Affairs, am I correct? But does this strike you as the kind of thing that could be kept under wraps forever? People don't disappear that easily. Those dead people still had scores of relatives and friends; it's ridiculous to think not a single one of them would find it suspicious. The only hope for concealing the real story was for it to be buried in a mass of conspiracy theories. And the reason the other theories fell away to reveal the truth was that operation by your External Affairs."

"Because we work better in the dark," I say in a daze.

"This investigation has been open for five years. Two years ago, we already had enough evidence to pressure President Han. None of us could've imagined that the old coot would've died so soon. The upcoming election spoiled our timing. But this information is still politically useful. We have no intention of letting it go to waste because some stupid employee of yours got possessed by a ghost and felt guilty all of a sudden."

"You have no intention of revealing the truth?"

"It'll be revealed someday. But if we simply tell people what happened, what do we get out of it? It'll just get filed away with all the other crimes committed by LK. This isn't even the worst one. Your company is responsible for the deaths and financial ruin of countless people, every single year. It's just so commonplace now that no one bats an eye. This case is special only because it's smeared with the guilt of Han Junghyuk. A huge point of leverage for us."

"So what are you going to do about it?"

"Work with Jaein. Ross Lee doesn't have a brain in his skull, and Han Suhyun is just a cheap knockoff of his dead grandfather. Not that either of them is a good target for blackmail."

"Kim Jaein has no intention of taking control of LK."

"The question of who becomes the figurehead of that organization is completely irrelevant to me. Ross Lee hardly lifts a finger and yet the company is perfectly fine. LK is slowly slipping the bounds of human control. And Jaein is the closest person in LK to the AI who really control the company. She's also a former college roommate of mine. Have you forgotten?"

Evidently, I had. I'd underestimated both Jaein and Nia Abbas and let them slip from my thoughts.

I look around the room we've been sitting in for at least an hour now. It's in the basement of a police station at the edge of the Gondal Quarter, a building undergoing expansion. The mayor's casual use of this room might mean that the Tamoé government is also involved. Or that the mayor is simply very good at eliciting cooperation from a wide range of allies.

The bathroom door opens, and Choi Gangwu steps out. He's dressed in plain clothes that the mayor's team had picked up for him at a nearby mall, and aside from some bruises here and there, his face is clean. Clean, but crumpled in anger and shame. He must've planned his death as a perfect ending. To shoulder the sins of the former president and burn away into

a pile of ash, cleansing the space elevator, purifying everything connected to Kim Jaein. But Nia Abbas has thwarted his
plans. Now that his adrenaline rush is abating, he's scared and
wants to see his sister in Youngwol, and he doesn't know what
his next step is—you don't need telepathy to see what's going
through his head.

"I killed a man," he says. As if he's holding out hope that the
murders will add weight to his pitiful existence.

"I know. But there's no way for us to prove that. Two men
from LK's Security Division just visited the scene of the crime
and there was a fire by the time they left an hour ago. The
drones put it out, but there won't be any bodies to speak of.
About fifteen minutes ago the news in Patusan reported the
death of an LK Space employee by the name of Haakon Larsen,
forty-three years old and a connoisseur of extreme sports—a
private plane crash near the Patusan harbor, his body lost to
the waves . . . Shark food by now, I'm sure. I'm just glad he at
least made a nutritious contribution to the local fauna."

"That doesn't change the fact that I'm a murderer."

"It was self-defense. If someone comes up to you with a
length of LK tube, of course you try to protect yourself from
being decapitated. One's own life is more important than the
lives of others. Always. Even the dead Mr. Larsen wouldn't
resent you for that. But let's talk about something more important right now. Who are you? Are you still Choi Gangwu?"

Choi Gangwu hesitates, then nods.

"Do you have the memories of the late President Han
Junghyuk?"

He nods again.

"Then do you know who killed Han Junghyuk?"

Incredulous, I shoot her a glance. The mayor is still looking relaxed, almost sleepy, completely oblivious to or uninterested in any signals I send.

Choi Gangwu, from his slouching stance, collapses onto a sofa across from us. His features begin to loosen up.

"How much do you know?" he asks.

"That President Han very likely died of a Soma-T overdose?" says the mayor. "That if this is true, he was killed using an astronaut drug that he himself had commissioned? Han Junghyuk's body was cremated without an autopsy, which means there's no way for us to prove it. But we did observe some classic Soma-T overdose symptoms in his behavior and appearance before he died. We could be wrong. But it's all so suspicious. If he had lived just one month longer, the situation regarding our investigation would've been very different from what it is now. Han Junghyuk knew that we knew about his disguising the murders as an accident, and he was getting ready to negotiate with us. The space elevator tower was complete and functioning perfectly. A new way into space for humanity was born, and that was enough for him. He wouldn't have cared if some other company had taken over the tower at that point, even if there were people in LK for whom that would've been intolerable. Let me ask again. Are our assumptions correct?"

"Y-yes, I think so."

"Do you know who killed him?"

"I don't. He always had a feeling that he would be assassinated. But my memories are incomplete. They're like collages made from ripped-up magazines. I think the last memory I have is from ten days before his death. The Australian National Opera had performed *Il Trovatore* here on their international tour. Renata Yoon had sung '*Stride la vampa*' and he had trembled and broken down in tears. He was already aware, then, that your people knew the truth behind the massacre. And he did feel guilt over it. I don't know what he was going to do about it. He was in a state of panic. From the outside he appeared to be enjoying his twilight years in splendor, but on the inside, things were getting worse and worse. I think he wanted to meet with you. But I don't know. These are what memories have been left to me, and important parts are missing. The rest of it is somewhere else. I do sometimes feel like I'm the former president, and I blurt out things he would've said, but that's the extent of it. I don't think he wanted me to have any more than that. That's my feeling."

He falls silent. He's run out of words, and the mayor doesn't seem interested in continuing her conversation with him. I glance at their faces and piece together the new information in my mind. The ridiculous thing is that there is nothing truly new here; the rumor that President Han had been poisoned started spreading a day before he actually died. Not to mention that old rumor that the agent used had been Soma-T. And that it was LK that had killed him. External Affairs itself had created parts of that rumor, so it would lose its credibility in circulation. I might have even been the one who'd made up the Soma-T part. My feeling, I recall, was that it fit a little too well, which would make people skeptical, helping to kill the rumor. If I wanted to, I could come up with a dozen fake arguments against what Choi Gangwu and Mayor Abbas had presented. But for what purpose? The whole point of this meeting is to verify the truth; my input would be useless here.

I ask, instead, "Who is this 'we' you keep mentioning?"

"The Patusan government. Not the Liberation Front or the Doran Party. Did you think we'd give up our sovereignty so easily and live out the rest of our days as LK's puppets? But I'm not here to preach some useless variant of Indigenous centrism or to kick LK out or nationalize the space elevator. Our aim is to have a properly functioning government. A country that can protect the people who live in it from the maniacal ambitions of the multinational corporation that dominates it. Where we don't have to ignore the fact that some chaebol president massacred dozens of our people and expects everything to be business as usual—the kind of country where we don't have to act grateful to that same man for sawing up a few murderers on our behalf and enacting *our* justice."

RETURN TO PATUSAN

Choi Gangwu and I are standing on the deck of a shuttle running from Tamoé to Patusan. The light rain stopped a moment ago but the sky is still overcast. Above the island of Patusan, purple stars slowly disappear into the clouds. Spiders carry parts for the *Dejah Thoris III,* a freighter for the Mars–Earth route. Once it's finished, it will be the largest manned spaceship ever built.

From the moment Patusan's space elevator became operational, things once possible only in the imagination began to materialize. Spaceships and space stations grew larger and more luxurious, on a scale previously unattainable. The number of asteroid-hunting spaceships surpassed 1,000 vessels last year; and next year a group of 1,500 supercompact spaceships will set off for Proxima Centauri, a forty-five-year voyage. Within five years, the first O'Neill cylinder colony will begin construction. Space is becoming more and more human-friendly, and the pace is dizzying.

Choi Gangwu, wearing a black baseball cap pulled so far down that the visor nearly covers his eyes, is staring at the faintly glimmering water. In profile he still looks somewhat like

himself, but from the front he's a completely different person.
I can tell he finds my face just as unfamiliar. It's different from
when he first met me and from when I left the hospital in Vientiane. I look younger and fatter, and calm to the point of stupid.

We're connected through our Worms now. I can hear and
see what he does, and vice versa. Unlike before, our Worms
aren't connected to Patusan's AI, which makes it feel like I'm
handcuffed to him in a glass prison cell.

The shuttle coasts toward the Patusan harbor. Passengers
start shuffling down toward the steps, and the freight robots
prepare for off-loading. Along the harbor, glass buildings
reflect the sunlight blazing yellow between the clouds.

We disembark and join the flow of workers making their way
into the new city. These aren't permanent-contract LK employees but people hired by an LK subcontractor on Pala called
Dobbs, Ltc.—the last vestige of the colonial Dobbs family, who
ruled Pala like royalty for two hundred years. On paper we,
too, are their employees: Eugene Hwang and Winston Hwang.
Brothers. Our altered faces have a family resemblance.

The Hwang brothers are both level H2—midlevel human
workers, in other words. At LK, midlevel humans need to go
to the bathroom from time to time, break for food, and have
problems concentrating, but they can handle fairly complex
work in the real world—much like cheap robots, in other
words. There are still places where human labor is cheaper
than robots, hence the H2s.

Most H2s work in the Viscera, the new city's inner workings,
where there are no windows. The name *viscera* is a little too
on the nose: two nuclear fusion generators, factories produc-
ing cables and spiders, transport tunnels, seawater processing,
and sewage. Every core functionality that makes life in Patu-

san City possible is handled in these guts, in other words. The bouquet of glittering jewels that constitutes the city's surface is merely the top layer.

"There will come a day when we won't need any of them," President Han Junghyuk had said, a year before his death, as he looked down at H2s on power loaders, constructing the rails that connect the second fusion plant to the harbor. "By then, human beings will do nothing productive at all. They'll just be lumps of desires. Andrei Kostomaryov says he's going to keep punching out those tin cans of his and fill the solar system with a hundred billion humans, but what are we going to do with so many of them? Our desires are basic and tedious. Should the creation of a zoo with a hundred billion space monkeys be the ultimate goal of our species?"

The president never mentioned such things in front of LK Space's biggest client—not that it would've made much difference if he had. There's still no way for Kostomaryov to build his O'Neill cylinders without going through us. It'll be another three decades, at least, before there's another space elevator, if it's built at all, and even then it'll likely be on Mars.

In our guise as H2s, we've been sent to a copper mine that was picked clean two centuries ago. Last time it was in use, before falling into disrepair for the past eighty years, this pitiful cave functioned as a bar and club. Now it's being remodeled as storage space for a museum. We do busywork designed to make us look like we're doing something important, and when the first lunch shift begins at eleven we slip out of the mine. We shower, change into civilian clothes, and melt into the crowds of the new city. A multicultural smorgasbord of space company employees, scientists, tourists, and service workers. People who live on the surface, unlike H2s.

We make our way through a troupe of Czech ballet dancers

doing a video interview, hotel robots acrobatically conveying luggage, a group of girls discussing the possible discovery of a third planetary system that can support life, and American tourists following an American flag drone, until we reach Rose Plaza—a large circle cut into the mountain, about two hundred meters in radius, and one of the few outdoor spaces in the city.

Standing in the middle of the crowd are three people: Mayor Nia Abbas, Andrei Kostomaryov, and Kim Jaein. They've been giving a talk since 11:00 a.m. about the Argos Project, a plan to send twelve telescopes into solar orbit between Jupiter and Pluto. The mayor is dispassionate, Kostomaryov is maniacal, and Kim Jaein keeps trying to pull him back down to Earth. Questions follow for Kim Jaein and Kostomaryov. While Kim Jaein speaks economically and precisely, Kostomaryov seems to regard each question as an opportunity to orate, sucking up all the time. Something about how the project will gift humanity with the largest eyes it's ever had, how it was a monumental achievement on par with traveling to different solar systems ourselves . . .

The event ends at 12:40. Kostomaryov takes the escalator to the airport and the mayor returns to city hall. Kim Jaein, along with two bodyguards, gets on the elevator meant for LK employees. We use our Daedalus Space Development Corp. IDs to follow them inside. The elevator begins to descend and we listen to the Percy Faith Orchestra's rendition of the theme from *A Summer Place*. This is some kind of nod from the Patusan AI to Kim Jaein, but I don't know the meaning behind it. Certain AI humor sails right over human heads.

Kim Jaein is wearing a black Reventon suit and her hair is tied up in a long ponytail. She has no makeup on, and her expression looks hard and determined. Because her face is so perfectly symmetrical, the mole on her right cheek appears all the more prominent. Her line of sight is fixed on the edge where the wall and ceiling meet, as if she's daring an invisible ghost up there to blink.

I glance at Choi Gangwu. He looks terrified, trembling as he stares down at his shoes. I suppose this is the first time he's ever seen Kim Jaein in person and not as President Han. If he were the main character in a novel, this is the part where he'd make love to her up and down with his words, but the real Choi Gangwu is simply pathetic. He's probably too lovestruck for thinking anyway.

The elevator doors open and we walk into the Nest. Kim Jaein strides toward a wall with a long screen and we split off toward the refreshments area. The face filling the large screen is that of Stella Siwatula, director general of the International Police Federation. Her voice can be heard only by Kim Jaein, but we already know what she's saying.

The Nest, or the spider base, is fifty meters below the sea's surface. Because of the "elevator" in space elevator, people tend to think the actual elevators are large boxes being hauled up and down cables, but each spider is actually an independent spaceship with highly specialized functions and shapes that vary from spider to spider—and these shapes and functions are getting more and more complex. Not all spiders are built to carry freight or passengers. Five of the spiders on the cable right now are for repairs or expansion. In between the passengers and the big "buses" and "trucks" that haul cargo are the little "builders," building out the cable with LK tubes. The first strand had quickly been joined by a second, and the cable has only been getting thicker and stronger ever since.

In the middle of the Nest is the elevator pillar. The spiders ride rails from here to the top floor before connecting with the cable. The actual cable starts at two hundred meters above the ocean surface, and there's a maintenance crew separate from cable maintenance that takes care of the pillar all the way to the top floor of the Nest.

Today three spiders have gone up the pillar and cable into space: two bringing parts to the *Dejah Thoris III* and one carrying food for the workers at the space station terminus. Just now, three flat teardrop-shaped spiders have arrived, meant for three astronauts who are headed for the *Clement,* a ship bound for Mercury. Workers are installing space capsules for the two-day journey ahead. Speed has gotten much better, but it's still a crucial disadvantage when it comes to space elevator travel. Anyone in a rush can opt for LK Space's other fine product: skyhooks.

DG Siwatula's face disappears, replaced by the new LK ad of the little girl riding a dragon to the stars. Kim Jaein converses with the workers inspecting the spider. I take a deep breath and approach them.

"Hello, Director Kim Jaein. My name is Tawahara Tazuya of the Daedalus Space Development Corporation. I believe I sent you an email yesterday?"

Kim Jaein nods. Slowly, we walk toward where Choi Gangwu is waiting. When my arm almost brushes against hers, Kim Jaein grimaces without trying to hide her reaction. I recall, too late, that she abhors all forms of physical contact.

My mind is racing. Me and Kim Jaein, her entourage behind us, the workers inspecting the spiders, and Choi Gangwu—I draw polygons upon polygons in my head. Just when I'm sure the polygons have coalesced into a perfect shape, I take out my gun, grab her waist with my left arm, and hold the weapon to her head.

"This is not a drill. If you value this woman's life, you'll leave immediately, all of you."

The Nest falls silent. In my grasp, Kim Jaein emits a series of wrathful moans, which finally convince the others I'm serious.

Slowly they move away from me. All except a single bodyguard, who holds his ground, staring at us. I move the barrel of the gun to Kim Jaein's neck and press the blue button above the trigger. With a *blip* the gun shoots a needle laced with tranquilizer, and Kim Jaein collapses in my arms. I wave the gun in the air at the stragglers and start to step backward. Once the last of her entourage is down the stairs, I activate the golem I've developed with my Worm and close all exits and communication channels. Kim Jaein, unconscious, has also lost control of her Worm; at least, that's what we're hoping people on the outside will believe.

I lay Kim Jaein down on a red sofa by the wall. Choi Gangwu tries to help but I wave him away. The least I can do for our hostage is make sure the lovesick Choi Gangwu never lays a hand on her.

The dragon-girl ad on the screen switches to a newscast and the AI anchor for Patusan News, Maxin Sunwoo, appears.

"A hostage situation at Patusan Tower is currently under way. Two infiltrators disguised as Tawahara Tazuya and Cho Minjung of Daedalus Space Development Corporation are holding LK Space Development Research Center Director Kim Jaein hostage at the Nest, police report. Their demands are yet unknown—

"New reports are now telling us that the hostage takers are in fact H2 workers Eugene Hwang and Winston Hwang, from labor subcontractor Dobbs. But these identities, too, seem manufactured, as not a single H2 worker at the company is aware of the existence of—"

The screen goes black. I feel the presence of someone behind me. The dead president's ghost? No. Something more substantial. I turn around.

Grinning down at me is a ghostly specter of Kim Jaein.

I glance at the Kim Jaein lying on the sofa behind the specter and then at the specter itself. According to Choi Gangwu's visual feed I'm not the only one seeing ghosts here. For a brief moment, I marvel at the structure of Kim Jaein's mind: all that goes on in there!

"And what the hell have you done to Ross Lee?" the ghost asks.

UNEXPECTED CULPRIT

The old president used to say that Ross Lee's only asset was his lack of existence. He took no real position in any argument, had no pack he ran with, no charisma, no leadership or vision. No advantages, but no disadvantages, either. He was stainless and harmless and concealed nothing. A little too interested in handsome young men, and a little whiny of late, after a recent divorce from his second and much younger husband, but even that flaw was minor compared to the whoppers circling the other higher-ups at LK.

"They'll install him in my position," the former president had predicted with disdain, "because the second I'm dead they'll want the company to run on inertia. It'll look nice for the shareholders, too."

Under Ross Lee, LK trundled along as expected. LK Space was hitting milestone after milestone, and a host of other things were happening around the LK Group—Koreans are nothing if not *dynamic*—but Ross Lee paid them no mind. If anything, the dead president was a livelier presence in the company than Ross Lee himself.

So imagine my shock when I learned that Green Fairy had unearthed evidence of Ross Lee meddling in Neberu

O'Shaughnessy's brain. Not only because I'd been so thoroughly bamboozled—that's not even the point here. I was annoyed at the fact that Ross Lee had turned out to be more than just an empty-headed yes-man. I don't know. Maybe I've been subconsciously enamored with his stupidity all this time.

"Adding Ross Lee into the equation does balance everything out," Sumac Graaskamp had said to me over the phone before our little foray into the Nest. "Han Junghyuk was worried that Han Suhyun and Security would betray him, and he'd built up his guard for that scenario. So who could have possibly broken through that barrier of suspicion to deliver the fatal poison to Han Junghyuk? Could the former president have predicted that his friend of thirty years would betray him so thoroughly?"

"But where's the motive? The man has no ambition or greed. They had to force him just to sit where he's sitting now."

"How should I know? I'm not a mind reader, Mac. But there's proof. In O'Shaughnessy's brain, LK Robotics, Security. He's the unsuspected culprit who's been able to fend off all suspicion from day one."

"Ross Lee never took control of Security. I know I told you we had no idea what was going on inside Security, but I do know Rex Tamaki. And he's not the kind of person who would take orders from the likes of Ross Lee. Tamaki is openly contemptuous of him. He would've been much more subtle about it if he were Ross Lee's man."

"You're right. It's all just a little too awkward and amateurish to be Tamaki. But Ross Lee *is* an amateur, which is why we found that trace of his handiwork in the first place. Neither Ross Lee nor Han Suhyun managed to take full rein of Security, but we forgot there are techies within Security who are loyal to their fellow techie-made-good Ross Lee. But the only way techies could help Lee out was to do it while cleaning up after

Security, because techies aren't field operatives. That explains that awkward, convoluted attempt to remove Choi Gangwu instead of just pushing him off a bridge somewhere. The only asset those techies could tap at the time was O'Shaughnessy."

"Who attacked us in Vientiane, then?"

"Not Security. It was another company Han Suhyun subcontracted with. You do know he hates you, right? It was an opportunity to kill you off without getting blood on his own people's hands. Do you think he'd give that up?"

In my head, I frantically test my hypothesis that Graaskamp is just baiting me, using Ross Lee as a sacrifice, an illusion dreamed up by Han Suhyun's people to lure us in the wrong direction; I try and I fail. The lack of polish about it all can't just be faked. And the stiltedness bears the markings of a certain personality. Ross Lee's, in this case.

Some ventriloquist's doll is suddenly going around killing people as if it were struck by Satanic lightning. But why? It's not like the CEO of LK has any real power anymore. And he has other things to do with his time. I try to come up with reasons why Ross Lee would secretly resent Han Junghyuk, but again I fail. Lee's not the kind of person to harbor such animosity.

"If you're so curious about it," says Graaskamp, "go ask Ross Lee yourself. I'll give you two days."

"And after two days?"

"The way he treated our employees, Mac. I can't let that slide. We have our own plans."

So Graaskamp ended up loaning me five of her Green Fairy workers, and exactly twenty-three hours later Choi Gangwu and I were having a chat with Ross Lee. It went down on the twelfth floor of the Millennium Hilton in Tehran, precisely one hour after a modern dance performance by a troupe LK was sponsoring.

And now, thirty-seven hours after *that,* we are face-to-face with the Kim Jaein specter at the Nest in Patusan.

The specter is uncannily identical to the real thing. If I hadn't known it was a digital projection created by my Worm, I would've thought she was real. The same appearance, the exact same shadows, even her footsteps match.

No—she *is* the real thing. The truest expression of Kim Jaein's thoughts and feelings is not the body lying on the sofa but the specter before me. And the specter looks more human than the corporeal Kim Jaein: wearing not a suit but loose, casual clothes in dark colors, purple bedroom slippers instead of shoes. A few strands of hair spring loose from her hairline. The center of her weight is on her left leg, her hands in her pockets. And she's smiling—the whole image is charming to an unsettling degree.

I'm unable to speak for a moment. Today's theatrics came courtesy of a script she and I had cowritten—but even as we collaborated we never shared that much information. Once the carefully written Act 1 of our little play came to a close, Act 2 was to be more of an improv situation. Act 2, therefore, was a trickier venture, and I'd been completely caught off guard by this unfamiliar side of Kim Jaein.

Finally overcoming my surprise, I tell her my story. About meeting Choi Gangwu, the murder attempt, the restoration of the dead president's memories, barging into a hotel room to meet Ross Lee. Whenever his own name is mentioned, Choi Gangwu's face turns red and his gaze drops to his feet.

"He didn't seem surprised," I remark to the Kim Jaein specter. "In fact, he seemed like he was waiting for us. Even if it took some effort to get up to his floor. He didn't withdraw his security or anything. But he must've known the moment would come someday—if not that day then some other day, with some other person. He was very serious about the crimes he'd committed. His conscience wouldn't allow him to ignore a crime of that magnitude, and he knew there would come a day where he'd have to confront his sins. That's when everything clicked into place. Ross Lee is just as obsessed with the aesthetics of a thing as Han Junghyuk was. That's how he was such an excellent engineer in his younger days. And why the two of them got along so well in their youth.

"But there was a hole in this narrative. Why did he do it? I was hoping Ross Lee would have a satisfying answer to this. Imagine if his motive for offing his friend of three decades, who was already near death, was to become head of LK just a few months faster. How disappointing would that be?

"Fortunately, that wasn't his answer. Ross Lee in fact had an excellent motive. One that dovetails perfectly with his character.

"At first, I'd thought it was connected with the Patusan government's plan to wrest their country back from LK. But Ross Lee knew nothing of that plan. He wasn't aware of the massacre that had taken place here, either. And his lack of awareness had been crucial. They needed a cheerleader for the brighter, idealistic side of LK. Han Junghyuk was of the mind that he alone should bear the weight of LK's sins, which is pretty narcissistic, if you think about it.

"But Ross Lee knew things regardless. He knew that Han Junghyuk was preparing the company for his death. This went beyond turning over his memories and objectives to AI. That was already being done in the open. President Han's real plan was to go beyond this—to fuse his mind with LK's AI, to become a god.

"I thought it was a joke. I'm no expert in the field, but I know such things are impossible. I checked again after our little talk with Ross Lee, and no breakthroughs have made it any more possible, as far as I can tell. But it's all a question of what the true objective is and how things are defined, isn't it? Many say that LK still runs on the dead president's will. But that will can of course be thwarted by the people who've survived him. To counter this, he needed to leave behind something living, something that could absorb new information and react to this new input with a free will. With this achieved, continuity of consciousness would matter much less. More important to him than continuity was ability. President Han tried to create a machine god that was like him but surpassed him in every capacity.

"Was it so terrible to become a god? Maybe not. Because ever since humankind made the first stone ax and lit the first fire, it has tried to surpass itself. A person who possesses a stone ax is a god to those who do not possess one themselves. If we look objectively at what President Han was trying to do, it is, in the end, just an extension of what he had tried to do all his life. Which in turn is simply an extension of something humanity has tried to do for as long as it's existed.

"The problem wasn't that President Han tried to become a god, the problem was that he tried to maintain control over LK even after his death. If he'd simply remained a god, no one would have blamed him. But when the dead start controlling the fate of the living, that's something else.

"Even without President Han's interference, the company's AI was growing in its influence. No matter how we try to prevent it, corporations like LK are destined to become one giant AI. In a hundred years, whole countries will likely meet the same fate. Humans may try to live according to free will, but we're all fated to disappear into the bowels of an AI behemoth. This is the future that awaits us, even if we try to resist. The only thing we can do here is buy a little time to adjust.

"Again, this is not the real problem. Everybody knows that LK's AI moves according to President Han's vision. It's best for the company that it does. But what if a group of prejudiced humans from a different generation tried to interfere with the AI's growth into a god? A dead person's vision and design are only matters of simple inertia, but a ghost with consciousness and a free will of its own—that's different, that's an abomination. This elderly ghost might claim that it's growing and learning and studying, but what's really at the end of that growth? And what happens when that decrepit ghost tries to take over the world's most important company?

"Ross Lee thought it had to be stopped. He poisoned the president, destroyed his Worm and all the data Han had wanted to upload. But that wasn't enough; somewhere, Ross Lee knew, in the vast network of LK, a backup of President Han's ghost might still be lurking. Consumed with his search to discover it, he neglected the company. I've mocked Ross Lee's laziness and ineffectualness for years, but it turns out he was the opposite of ineffectual, that his apparent laziness was the by-product of his desperate, constant search.

"Then along came this guy, Choi Gangwu. Ross Lee was practically the only person who knew that Han Junghyuk was in love with you. He was also one of the few people who picked up on the physical resemblance between Choi Gangwu and Anton Choi. He even used the techies at Security to plant bio-bots in the brains of Green Fairy employees. The LK Robotics techies who contributed to this mess had been hired by Ross

Lee even before he killed President Han. This is not some great coincidence—there are simply too few people in the world who have these particular skills. In any case, it was only a matter of time before Choi Gangwu's secret would be leaked.

"But Ross Lee must have asked himself: Is that all there is to it? All President Han wanted was to transfer a bit of his memory to some young man and to try to seduce Kim Jaein? Was his dead friend's plan that comically simple? He had to be sure, which is why he got the company to hire Choi Gangwu.

"Creating zombies out of Green Fairy employees using biobots makes perfect sense in that regard. He needed field operatives that he could control and had only techies in Security at his disposal. Normally you'd just hire a subcontractor, but I can understand the urge to use his own trusted technology, even if it meant breaking a few rules. I know he seems benign now, but Ross Lee was quite the mad scientist in his day. We're talking about a man who bioengineered a creature twice the size of the average blue whale to produce LK tubes in a factory. He wasn't such a cruel person to begin with, but once he got it into his head that he was on a mission to save humanity, he started to think in terms of expendable lives.

"Ross Lee soon found himself beset by more and more complications in his plan. External Affairs got involved, and O'Shaughnessy was exposed. When O'Shaughnessy was killed in an attempt to harvest Choi Gangwu's Worm, Lee went into a panic. The situation kept getting bigger and eventually caught Rex Tamaki's eye at Security. Han Suhyun, tipped off by Tamaki's intel, was beginning to smell a rat as well. Lee had to dispose of the new young employee, since he was clearly a part of his dead friend's conspiracy, but unlike Security's field operatives, Lee didn't have the means to wrap it up neat and tidy. He had no choice but to follow the twisted paths of the conspiracy, like in an Agatha Christie classic, because to him that was the simplest way forward.

"'Junghyuk never died, you know,' Lee said to me. 'At least, he's still alive to me. No matter how much I tried to kill him, a part of him stayed alive somewhere in the company. It was as if my attempts to kill him were actually prolonging his life inside me. I don't know how much of me is Ross Lee and how much of me is Han Junghyuk.'

"I said, 'Does this mean you've given up your search for him?'

"'No,' he told me. 'If anything, I see his plan more clearly now. What would Junghyuk have done to prevent someone like me from killing him off? Where would he have hidden the data that contained his mind, the data he would've grafted onto the AI after getting rid of everyone like me? Isn't it obvious, if you think about it for a moment?'

"'You mean the space station at the end of the elevator?'

"He shook his head. 'No, it's too busy there. It's way, way up, even beyond the space elevator station. It's in the counterweight.'"

WAKE THEM

"Did Green Fairy kill Ross Lee?" the specter asks.

"No, why would they? When he's so much more useful to them alive, especially with the new intel they had on him. What the news report said is true. Ross Lee injected himself with four times the OD level of Soma-T and died. Not even from guilt. Yes, a few people died because of him, his childhood friend Han Junghyuk, for instance, but he believed to the end that he did it all for the good of humanity. The reason Ross Lee killed himself is something different. It was heartbreak. Four days ago, his second ex-husband walked away, dismissing Lee's attempt at a reconciliation. Lee didn't die because he lost the war, he died for love. He cared more about love and pride than about the fate of humanity. Not that someone like you would understand."

I immediately regret saying that last bit. But in that moment I realize why I've always hated Kim Jaein so much. It's her attitude. That feeling that she's always judging and mocking us for our little desires and emotions and such. Like she's some kind of alien. She may have the manners and superficial niceties of a civilized human, but she's constantly surrounded by a miasma of chemical something or other.

I don't know, though. The specter standing before me doesn't seem too scandalized by what I've just said. Unlike the Kim Jaein I've known all these years, she is, if anything, looking sympathetically at me, nodding even.

It's Choi Gangwu who is scandalized. It's like I flipped a switch. His limp form springs back to life, his face bright red.

"I'm sorry," I say, flustered, "I shouldn't have said that."

"It's fine."

The specter smiles. She sits down on the sofa where the corporeal Kim Jaein still lies. Not because she's tired of standing, obviously, but perhaps because she wants to change her position to fit the flow of the story. The cushion doesn't budge as she sits, making it seem like a sofa made of rock.

Look, Mr. Gildong. Star stuff.

Choi Gangwu had claimed that this was one of "his" memories of Kim Jaein; but there's no way she said such a trite and sentimental thing. Would even the specter before me be capable of saying it? Did she ever allow herself to be as ridiculous in front of President Han?

"Did you ever call the dead president Mr. Gildong?"

Kim Jaein shakes her head.

"So it's not a real memory?"

"I'm sure it's a real memory. I'm just not the person in that memory, that's all." She grins, but there is no mirth in her expression. "Half of his memories of me—no, maybe more— are made up. He needed fiction to fill in the blanks. There are so many versions of me because of it. A cuter, lovelier version. A crueler, colder version. A sexier, seductive version. Even a version that's more me than my own self.

"That in itself isn't strange. Everyone lives with fantasies of their objects of affection. And we live in an age when we can project and materialize such fantasies. Do you think I'm not aware of the heinous number of fanfics based on me? The only difference with Han is that he had access to incredible-technologies. Technologies he utilized to spin fantasies of me.

"President Han Junghyuk never forced himself on me, nor did he demand affection. He was always polite and kept his distance. His head was so full of fantasies he didn't need to force me to do anything. I learned about them quite recently. Through interrogating the Patusan AIs.

"The memories injected into Choi Gangwu were probably modified. Or selected from his favorite memories. But I think what really happened was that he had failed to let go of a few made-up memories, and those had slipped through into the set he preserved. I wonder if that 'Mr. Gildong' memory was that special to him."

"He wanted an idealized version of himself to combine with you."

Kim Jaein frowns. "I don't think so. He just wanted to leave behind an idealized portrait of himself. To retain the most beautiful feelings and desires that he possessed, from his perspective anyway, and let them live on. I don't think he even imagined he would 'combine' with me in any way."

She stands up. She turns toward Choi Gangwu, who's still idling there like he's been turned to stone, but instead of approaching him she puts her hands in her pockets and begins to pace around the room with a light gait, almost dancing. Choi Gangwu stares at her face, which has the carefree expression of a child, but then his own face flushes and his gaze drops once more.

"Don't you think I'm right, Mr. Choi Gangwu?"

The man nods, slowly. As if admitting defeat in a war that hasn't even begun.

This is not going according to plan at all. Not that I'd calculated for every possibility, but still; I had not expected Kim Jaein to have conquered Choi Gangwu so easily. I'd thought the sight of her actual self would disenchant him, that he would have retained at least some of his faculty for self-control.

The specter is going on about things I had expected her to say. But where was the robotic woman I'd once known? Where did she pick up this attitude, these expressions, these gestures, this voice? Was the coldness I had seen on the battlefields of LK an armor all along? Where did they come from, these unfamiliar characteristics that were throwing a wrench into the gears of my plans?

Frustrated, I jump into the space between them.

"So what? What's the point of everything we've gone through until now, why did we have to put on this insufferable act to meet you in the first place?"

Kim Jaein steps back and takes a good look at us both; she is the peak of an isosceles triangle, Mr. Hapless and me the other two corners. This little ghost is smaller than both of us but is starting to dominate us with ease. Her constant, almost child-like smile does nothing to dispel this effect.

"Because there's still something you need to do. The vision in Choi Gangwu's head is a portrait, yes, but it's also a key. My uncle seems to have cut up his mind like a jigsaw puzzle and hidden it away in the counterweight. We must quickly put the pieces back together. Because if Ross Lee was able to figure it out, Suhyun oppa is sure to follow."

"What happens if Han Suhyun finds out first?"

"Oppa will destroy Han Junghyuk's mind hiding in the counterweight and try to use some scarecrow or other to consolidate his power at LK. Now that Ross is out of the picture, there's no one to stop him. And Suhyun oppa is the absolute worst person to lead LK at this juncture.

"Ross acted as if my uncle's mind combining with the company AI would be the beginning of some apocalypse. But that isn't the case. Don't you think we've been preparing for that eventuality? President Han's mind and will merging with an AI doesn't mean we'll suddenly fall under his dictatorship. What's more likely to happen is it will stop my deluded oppa from damaging the company at a historically crucial moment for humanity, when we're about to take our first steps into the stars."

"And what does Nia Abbas have to do with all this?"

"The most important thing for Han Suhyun is LK. The space elevator itself is maybe fourth down on his list. But to Han Junghyuk, LK was not that much of a priority, it was the space elevator that mattered. He didn't even care if the elevator changed ownership, as long as it remained intact and operational. As for the Patusan government, they would much prefer dealing with the old president, Han Junghyuk, than with Han Suhyun because they'd have more of an upper hand."

"But what's the rush to get to the counterweight? Knowing the old president, he must have booby-trapped the thing—and whatever booby trap is up there is probably smarter than Han Suhyun. I bet this shy fellow here isn't even the only key he left behind. If he gets killed off, ten other men will probably come find you and stare at you with puppy-dog eyes."

"You're right. But there's no reason to wait and see if that happens, is there?"

SOMEONE HAS TO GET IT DONE

I wonder, momentarily, if the specter in front of me is not the real Kim Jaein after all. Of course I do: the real Kim Jaein is unconscious, and for all I know I'm interacting with some AI or someone imitating Kim Jaein. This whole melodramatic theater piece itself might be a plot cooked up by someone who has it in for Kim Jaein—I'm suddenly overwhelmed with suspicion.

But nothing would change if that were the case. This is our only available exit. Choi Gangwu must make his way up to the counterweight. It's the only ending that fits in this narrative. As long as we make it up there, it doesn't matter if this Kim Jaein is the real one or not.

I've never given too much thought to the counterweight at the end of the space elevator. It's a crucial component of the design, of course. The counterweight pulls at the cables with centrifugal force, maintaining the structure of the elevator. As the cable became two strands and each strand thickened, the lumpy counterweight, which was started with the remains of a captured asteroid exploited for mining, grew larger and larger as well. Next they sent trash from the fixed-orbit station up there, contributing to its growth. It's now a mess of space debris and discarded cables, a veritable floating junkyard. And now that there's stable gravity up on the station, thanks to centrifugal force, it will eventually extend toward the counterweight itself—but not yet. It's still too far, and the fixed-orbit station is already acting as a hub for humans and cargo escaping Earth's gravity well.

At the moment, the counterweight is populated solely by robots. A world of small machines peacefully cleaning and stacking debris and rocks and trash, with no interference from humans.

And it's a great place to hide something. Every trip up the space elevator leaves a record, and the spiders' movement is under constant watch. Skyhooks and rockets can make it up there more or less undetected, disguised as ships carrying space debris, but it's still extremely difficult to enter the counterweight. Even if someone somehow pulled it off, they'd instantly lose themselves in the maze of junk and would starve to death or run out of battery before finding what they're after. Then the robots would scoop up their remains and stack them with the rest of the trash. Only those who know their way around, who know how things work in the counterweight, could succeed in such a treasure hunt. There's an almost fairy-tale-like quality to the whole enterprise. Which very much bears the imprimatur of the late President Han.

Choi Gangwu is busy putting on a space suit. It's his first time since company training, but he's adept at plugging in the urinal tube and attaching the artificial nerve pads to the lining. Is he tapping into President Han's memories, of the five trips up the elevator he made in his lifetime? I used to think I could read President Han's mind like an open book, but now I'm not so sure. How much have his reanimated memories altered the brain of Choi Gangwu? And are those memories, truly, all that's been reawakened?

Kim Jaein gives the signal and Choi Gangwu steps into a

vertical capsule inside the spider. Detecting his weight, the spider slowly turns the capsule horizontal and adjusts the other two empty capsules, centering its gravity. Following Kim Jaein's orders, I seal the spider.

One of the exits of the Nest opens. A young, muscular woman with short hair comes in pushing a folding wheelchair. This is the nurse they sent on Kim Jaein's order, which I conveyed word for word. The nurse hasn't been working at LK for long, which means she has no brain augmentations. I wave my gun at her, pointing her toward the body on the sofa. The nurse does a quick inspection of the corporeal Kim Jaein and hoists her down into the wheelchair. They enter the Nest living quarters and I lock them inside. I glance back. Kim Jaein's specter looks more at ease now. Even though this was her plan from beginning to end, she must have felt some tension, seeing her body so vulnerable like that. Not that she could have asked for safer accomplices than some old queen and Don Quixote here.

From the view on the monitor, the inside of the spider resembles an iron maiden. Choi Gangwu looks terrified. Then, suddenly, his features relax. Kim Jaein has remotely injected him with Soma-T. His sense of time will slow down. An unavoidable measure, seeing as how he's going to be in there for the next three days. It doesn't matter. What I need now is not Choi Gangwu but his Worm, and unlike its host, his Worm runs at normal speed. I've got to use every asset I have right now if I'm to survive what's coming.

The cover slides shut and the spider enters the elevator column. Its edges hook up to a pair of rails. The column door closes, and I can hear the spider ascending.

My Worm opens wide; Kim Jaein is feeding me information on Patusan. I can see the city and the structure of the space elevator, right before my eyes. I can see the spider containing

Choi Gangwu climbing slowly up the rails, the station AI gearing up to connect the spider with the elevator cable. I see the movements of spectators, reporters, police, and LK employees. Security's drones swarm around the spider. I see the cappuccino machine in the basement cafeteria is broken. I see a urinal being flushed in a police station bathroom. I glimpse the face of a missing child. Clouds of butterflies on CCTV. There is so much information being poured into me that I marvel at how my brain remains intact. But of course, it would take a lot more to break an LK Worm. All this input fades into impressions.

I mark every Security operative resident in the city with a blue dot. Among them, I isolate Alexander Mtunz Tamaki and draw a blue circle around him. He'd been in Tamoé until recently, but now he's circling Patusan on a Hummingbird. I can't infiltrate their communications, but using the movement of the blue dots I can guess at what they're up to. They're on the offensive. They've realized what's going on, and their objective is clear. Block the spider before it connects to the elevator cable.

I leap onto the employee elevator. Kim Jaein doesn't follow. I don't even know if she's still in the Nest; it doesn't matter. The specter was necessary only for psychological manipulation. Choi Gangwu and I are now under her control.

I'm ascending the elevator at nearly the same speed as Choi Gangwu's spider. I extend scores of unseen feelers from inside the elevator and enter the Patusan system. I block every approach Security's drones can make on the spider. It's not enough. Blue dots speed toward the rails, and the spiderweb-like internal security system of the elevator is beginning to rouse.

An explosion. Thirty Security drones have broken into the vertical shaft and are flying inside. If even one of them touches the rail, the spider will freeze midway. But Kim Jaein is quick.

She gives me passwords to eleven of the drones, and they come under my control. Now I can fend off the other nineteen, but I can't just fire at them indiscriminately or I might damage the rail. I use three of my drones to shoot nanomissiles at the enemies beneath me and engage the others in drone-to-drone combat. One by one, they start to fall. I release the gnats—forty mini-drones, the size of flies, swarm out and kamikaze into the enemy craft. Because the mother drone that normally controls them has crashed, I have to guide each gnat myself using Choi Gangwu's Worm; even with the very different touch required to maneuver the smaller drones, my own Worm quickly "learns" the technique and I'm instantly an old hand. When the last enemy drone has been shot down, I still have two of mine left.

With a loud clang, a piece of railing ricochets off the spider— 3.2 kilometers up the track I can see the Security operative who's done the damage with a mini-missile. I steer my drones up and blow the bastard's head off just as he's aiming a second missile. His body and brains glance off the spider as they fall. I check the rail's condition: there's a gap of about a meter where his missile struck, and a rail is twisted where segments have broken off. Nothing the spider can't handle—it can climb up to four meters using just one rail.

An alarm goes off in my mind. One of the five railguns attached to the top floor is in motion. These guns were originally installed to protect the elevator. Structurally, they're not able to fire on the cable or the spiders—as far as I know, at least. But now the railguns smash free of their concrete supports. They turn at dramatic angles. Some hidden feature, apparently, activated by Security. I run a check on the link between the guns and Security, to see where it leads back to: Rex Tamaki.

Why would he have installed such a feature in the first place? Sure, blowing away a spider with a railgun is a perfectly plausible scenario. But that goes against the subtle political tactics Tamaki has always relied on at LK. If Choi Gangwu dies, Han Suhyun will be thrilled. But using the railguns' hidden features to shoot down a spider would create headaches for both Han Suhyun and Security. Suhyun's competitors at LK would pounce, and Tamaki, too, would find his position in peril. And there's really no need for Tamaki to be so self-sacrificingly loyal to Han Suhyun. It's not like he took an oath to serve him, and Security can always find some other figurehead to support. Bringing President Han back to life wouldn't be the end of Tamaki's career. So why on Earth are you doing this, Alexander? Do you know something I don't?

I open my eyes, which I'd kept closed this entire time. My elevator is at 3.67 kilometers, twenty meters below the top floor. I take out my gun, disengage the safety. The door opens and I leap out onto the top floor. Gunshots, a grazing wound across my left arm. Processing the visual info sent by Kim Jaein, I run forward and shoot twice. Two screams, the targets disappear— but I don't hear any thuds. Their bodies are in freefall. I pick up the mini-missile launchers the bodies had been using before they went overboard. There's no sign of Tamaki's Hummingbird. How do these weapons even work? But I don't have to wallow in ignorance long, as Kim Jaein floods my Worm with instructions. I still don't see the Hummingbird, but there's no need to. Peering through Kim Jaein's godlike eye on the skies, I take aim and fire a missile. The Hummingbird explodes; and the body of the man I'd once salivated over is shattered among the fragmented titanium.

The contorted railguns bow their heads. Kim Jaein has finally managed to hack into them. I hear a familiar harpsichord sound. The spider carrying Choi Gangwu has hooked onto the cable and is making its ascent.

COUNTERWEIGHT

As the spider makes its way up, the low, muffled sound grows louder and louder, until it's clearly the theme for *A Summer Place*. *Ta ta ta ta ta ta, ta ta ta ta ta ta, ta ta ta ta ta ta, ta ta ta ta ta ta* . . . Six times the tune repeats, and by the third Choi Gangwu feels he's going to lose his mind.

From the outside, it appears as if Choi Gangwu has been taking a sixty-hour nap in his space suit. But he's been awake all the while. It's only his sense of time that has altered. Sixty hours in the real world was only fifteen minutes for him. The outside world has been whirling at such a clip that he can barely make out what's happening. His lagging mind can't keep up with his physical reflexes.

With his brain, as with mine, connected by Worm to Kim Jaein, he absorbed everything that was going on with the Patusan space elevator outside his spider, only to let it go a moment later. Everything I'd done, risking my life to save the spider, flashed before him in less than a second.

Unable to process the dealings of people, Choi Gangwu turned his attention to the world beyond. Space moved more slowly than people. The capsule screen showed the view from the spider's external cameras: in a flash the sky turned dark;

stars appeared and drifted into an arc in unison. While the celestial firmament rotated two and a half times, Mars and Jupiter moved at an even slower pace. Somewhere around the fourth loop of the *A Summer Place* theme, he passed the fixed-orbit station; at the sixth loop, his screen turned blank.

Choi Gangwu now stares into the "ground," lying flat on his stomach. The capsule's angle hasn't changed, but gravity had slowly weakened as he ascended, and the moment he passed the station the centrifugal force had begun to drag him away from Earth.

The capsule stops and the spider's canopy opens. Choi Gangwu attempts to get out, but his body refuses to respond. There's a sharp pain in his neck. His space suit has just administered another injection, this time to counter the effects of Soma-T. The seventh loop of the *A Summer Place* theme peters out.

Choi Gangwu finally manages to disembark from the spider. He's been stuck in there for sixty hours, but the capsule has been providing him with a continuous stream of water and nutrients, and there's nothing amiss with his health. Except for the moment or two he needs for his muscles and reflexes to normalize. He walks around the spider, adapting himself to the lighter but steady artificial gravity of the counterweight.

My Worm brings up a 3D map. Choi Gangwu and the spider are currently in the metal trash pyramid, where bales of crushed spaceships and satellite debris wrapped in cables are configured into a maze just wide enough for one person wearing a space suit. While this seems an awfully considerate design, the passageways are meant not for humans but for robots.

A truck robot, shaped somewhat like a scorpion, approaches the spider. It ignores Choi Gangwu, who flinches in its presence, and sticks two pipes into the spider's dashboard. The interior of the spider flashes to some indecipherable rhythm.

Choi Gangwu paces slowly. He doesn't know where he is or where he's going, but that doesn't matter. He looks up. Earth was there somewhere. But the only other things he can see are stacks and stacks of the metal garbage of the counterweight.

Footsteps. Despite the total vacuum, he can "hear" footsteps and the swooshing of garments. Kim Jaein's specter. It's walking beside him, arms stretched to the sides, like it's on a tightrope. Ponytail bouncing.

Where should I go now?

Just wait. The system will take care of it. All you have to do is react appropriately.

Choi Gangwu walks on and waits. The only thing he can feel is the staleness of the air inside his space suit and the ache from his urinal tube. *Pathetic,* he thinks to himself, of himself.

A flash of yellow light, like a lightbulb in an old movie. Not a true light. Augmented reality—superimposed on the real reality he sees with his naked eyes. The two are now in a large room with old-fashioned wallpaper. There's a smell of baby powder and milk, and through the open window, Russian music. A large toy airplane dangles from a thick rope in the middle of the ceiling. Choi Gangwu bats at it with his space-suit-gloved hand, and the airplane comes to life, snaps its rope, and flies out the window.

Now Choi Gangwu is riding first-class in an airplane. He's not wearing a space suit. Instead, he's in a cheap suit that doesn't quite fit him. Next to him is a middle-aged man who has dozed off. Choi Gangwu pulls his personal seat screen toward him and switches on the mirror function. Han Junghyuk, in his early twenties. Shabby, effete. His hair removal surgery must have been poorly administered because his five o'clock shadow is patchy, and his sleeve has a smear of mustard.

Everything speeds up in that moment. Everything seen and heard becomes the seed of a chain reaction, and those seeds grow exponentially. In an instant, the many fragments that compose Han Junghyuk's life arrange themselves in Choi Gangwu's brain. Most of it is familiar, at least to anyone who's read any books by Han Sahyun, Jaein's mother, or seen her plays. Except they are all in Han Junghyuk's first-person perspective. Choi Gangwu watches Han Junghyuk's whole life through his eyes. Han Junghyuk going to Seoul with President Han Bugyeom. Being bullied by Han Bugyeom's sons. Only Han Sahyun treats him with affection, and mostly because she knows it will piss off her oppas. Han Junghyuk leans on Han Sahyun, begins to learn more about the world he finds himself in. He cackles as he pores over her books; and when the bomb explodes at the funeral, he cries for two days until his eyes are swollen. Following the guidelines of the late President Han Bugyeom, he becomes the head of LK. Then one day, Kim Jaein rears her nonchalant little head, entering the Han family.

At first, her precocity is adorable, but there is something more to this thirteen-year-old. He knows she doesn't have a drop of blood in common with Han Sahyun, but her attitude and cadence resemble hers all the same. She grows into a personality of her own, nothing like Han Sahyun's or Kim Lena's. She speaks of the stars and the development of the human mind. Han Junghyuk, despite his crippling guilt, feels love for this niece with whom he has no biological connection. And because this is a love he can never, ever hope to be requited, the repressed emotions in his brain start leaking out in all sorts of contradictory ways. Kim Jaein comes to symbolize everything that is valuable to Han Junghyuk. She is his daughter, his teacher, his student, his muse, a goddess from an old black-and-white movie. President Han's universe belongs to Kim Jaein. He had no interest in space or the space elevator before, but now they are everything to him. Because they are everything to *her*. Because she wants to leave the world behind and travel through space more than she wants anything else in the world. The late president decides nothing must stand between the child and her dreams, least of all the beggars digging dirt for their food where the space elevator should be standing. Their filthy fishing boats and whores have nothing to do with the beautiful towers he will build.

Then, from nowhere, Adnan Ahmad's large face pops into Choi Gangwu's memories, like a ghost in a haunted house attraction, and everything President Han has worked for turns to foam.

Choi Gangwu and Kim Jaein are now standing in the collapsed tunnel in Patusan. There are bodies crushed under rubble, smoke and dust fill the air. It looks less like the actual scene of an accident and more like a movie set or a videogame.

Before them is the figure of President Han, wearing a green cardigan over his hospital gown, shining white and standing in a painfully twisted posture. His face is full of suffering. Like a man caught in a nightmare of his own making.

Choi Gangwu glances to his side, where the Kim Jaein specter is staring down at the late president, her expression as cold and dispassionate as the marble bust of some divine judge. The Kim Jaein of before, with her easygoing grins, with her penchant for pragmatism and compromise, has disappeared. No— this is not the face of a judge. This harshness isn't founded in justice. It's some kind of extreme fastidiousness, combined with a ruthless sense of balance.

I finally understand. She isn't here to reanimate Han Jung-hyuk's mind. She's here to kill him. To erase him. For the same reasons that Han Junghyuk found it unforgivable that the three lawyers would blemish his space elevator with rape and murder, Kim Jaein could not forgive him for the massacre. The elevator needed to be beautiful and pristine, and the blemish that is Han Junghyuk rubbed out. The mind in control of humanity's passage into the stars needed to be wiped clean of human flaws.

Kim Jaein's excuses in the Nest over the past few days had all been a show for the ghost of President Han Junghyuk. The president had tried to carry over the best and wisest parts of himself, to forge a new mind from them, but no matter how much more noble and beautiful and clean, he would never be free of the deeds he'd committed in life or his desires. Meanwhile Kim Jaein had pretended all along that her aim was to free the ghost from the counterweight—but what we instead achieved was to make Han Junghyuk confess all his sins. And no matter how many uncomfortable memories he had rid himself of, the sins would still stick to him like iron dust to a magnet.

The ghost of Han Junghyuk stares the two of them down, his crumpled face all but twitching with grotesque sadness. But Kim Jaein pays no mind to his suffering. It is impossible she is unaware that all the beauty and sincerity before her is as staged as a Verdi aria. The digital ghost of the counterweight does not bear a truly "natural" expression, and Kim Jaein knows too much about the dead man to be fooled by such theatrics.

Han Junghyuk's ghost speaks.

My baby. I know you've come here to kill me. But I am glad we get to meet one last time.

His smile is bitter, yet somehow a little sweet. Who could've imagined this man was capable of such a smile? Realistic as it seems, though, there's still no way it's anything but theatrics.

President Han raises his left hand. It holds a toy laser gun, stickers messily applied all over it, the kind either of them could have plucked from the childhood memories we've just traversed. He waves the gun as if saying goodbye, puts the muzzle in his mouth, and pulls the trigger.

He explodes. All the memories that had constituted the old man shatter in an instant. The fragments, like a flock of butterflies, flit off into the air before dissolving into nothing.

A CREDIBLE LIE

"Winston Hwang's real name is Damon Chu. He's part of LK Space's External Affairs, but he works from home, so we've never met him in person."

I am talking to Director Stella Siwatula, who's staring at me with eyes full of suspicion. I can't tell whether that glare is because she's stuck on a call with some corporate serf who's beneath her notice, or whether she's truly suspicious. Who knows if she still remembers the face I had fifteen years ago, when I last dealt with her, but I don't bother dwelling on such a thought for now.

I go on. "We have many such employees. As long as they do their job and go about their responsibilities, we don't care where they work. As for Eugene Hwang, his accomplice, we haven't been able to identify him yet. The police are looking into it, but he seems to have had his identity laundered by an expert.

"It appears to us that when he was alive, President Han Jung-hyuk used Damon Chu as one of his assistants. We're not sure what he tasked him with specifically, but he seems to have many of the late president's artworks and even furniture in a storage container facility in Bandar Seri Bagawan. Most of the items are hot, and a few have already been returned to their rightful owners. LK is committed to cooperating with the Indonesian police to return the rest.

"To sum up the situation so far, Damon Chu seems to have thought the dead president had hidden some kind of valuable object or information in the space elevator's counterweight. He must have believed he knew where it was. We're not sure where he got this information, nor were we able to confirm whether it was true. But the fifteen thousand in International Credits, taken out in cash just before the hostage situation, was likely payment for this information.

"We could not determine what it was, exactly, that Damon Chu found in the counterweight. But we do know that within one hour of having arrived there, he took an emergency escape pod out. The pod landed in the Indian Ocean and our company seized it, but the occupant had already escaped. We're trying to determine what happened in the counterweight by going through our robots' data, but we're doubtful we'll find anything of substance. The counterweight, you must understand, is not the kind of place we expect thieves to strike.

"His accomplice, who went by the name of Eugene Hwang, escaped in a second spider as soon as Damon Chu arrived at the counterweight. Our records show the access hatch of this spider opening and closing at the forty-two-kilometer mark, and we estimate he also made his escape using a single-passenger aircraft. The spider has been handed over to the police, who are investigating."

There are very few lies. Eugene Hwang's identity was indeed laundered by an expert, namely me. The spider's access hatch did open and close at forty-two kilometers above sea level, and a damaged flying robot had been dumped out, whereupon the robot slowly descended to ten meters above the ocean before splitting in two and crashing into the waves. Rescuing Choi Gangwu using the escape pod was a little trickier, with the presence of the Space Police and all. But Sumac Graaskamp has the perfect magic trick for every occasion.

"We're still looking into the mayhem that occurred in the beginning of the hostage situation. The railgun seems to have been activated by the recently deceased head of Security, Alexander Tamaki. All the employees who tried blocking the spider's ascent during the incident have been identified as members of the Wolf Pack, a select group in Security especially loyal to Mr. Tamaki, and they had evidently been given orders to prevent Damon Chu from reaching the counterweight at all costs. We are still investigating the reason they were so invested in this objective. Please disregard the rumors circulating on the Internet. When we say we don't know something, we really do mean it."

Most of those conspiracies were of our own making. And there are a few I wouldn't mind adopting as the official explanation. We haven't yet decided which we'll settle on as the final narrative. I just want a fairly honorable ending for Tamaki and his thugs. Something to keep people from looking upon us with more than the necessary amount of suspicion.

Director Siwatula begins her dogged interrogation. Questions that appear harmless on the surface are filled with traps. The traps trigger a warning from my Worm whenever they're detected, or from Kim Jaein's Worm, I should say, which is feeding me these analyses. The closest I come to falling into one is with Neberu O'Shaughnessy. I insist I know nothing about the whole affair. Even a made-up answer would be suspicious here, as there's nothing more suspicious than having a well-prepared answer for everything.

I read off my answer to her final question as the words form on my retina, courtesy of my Worm: "Director Kim Jaein is alive and well. She was locked in a room with a nurse named Para Wardani from the beginning of the hostage situation and there was no contact with the hostage takers. You can get the rest of that story from Nurse Wardani if you'd like. We've come to the conclusion, based on all the information we have, that no harm was intended to come to Director Kim. The hostage situation was created by Damon Chu to distract authorities from his real goal. Eugene Hwang used some hologram or whatnot to make it seem like he was in the Nest, but it's the kind of illusion one can pull from within a spider. The two people were, in other words, riding their spiders the whole time.

"Any other questions, Director?"

ET NOUS, NOUS RESTERONS
SUR LA TERRE

"He says he can't remember."

"Can't remember what?"

"Kim Jaein's face."

"What?"

Sumac Graaskamp frowns. "Like I said. He can't remember Kim Jaein's face. He can remember everything except for that. I showed him a photo of her and he said she didn't look familiar. That he had never seen her before and could feel nothing. How broken can a brain get? He said it felt like a corner of his brain had exploded when the ghost of Han Junghyuk was killed."

"What's the point of forgetting just her face?"

"You know she hates it when someone likes her like *that*. Romantically, I mean. She can't stop people from loving her, but she can make it very annoying to love her."

Graaskamp and I are walking on the beach by the old half-submerged city. The day has long since turned to night and there's a chill in the air. We'd spent the last two days putting together Eugene Hwang's dead body. Not that anyone believes the case is truly solved, but we have to at least allow the Indonesian police to save face. Damon Chu will go down as missing. I always liked the story of D. B. Cooper—the man who flew all the way to the other side of space to steal an unknown treasure, only to disappear. Our story is even better than that. I'm just sad I wasn't the one who wrote it. The true author here, I suppose, is the situation, which wrote itself.

Eugene Hwang's story, meanwhile, isn't too bad, either. But the true story of how I escaped the airtight Nest is almost boring. When the police came, I'd simply hidden myself in one of the city's many subterranean tunnels, and thanks to Kim Jaein ordering the Patusan AI to ignore my presence, I could slip away as if I were invisible. The whole time I was pulling off this "hostage" trick, my avatar had successfully fulfilled its function at work, and whatever it couldn't do Miriam had filled in for, which meant no one had noticed I wasn't where I was supposed to be. Even if they had, they'd sound like fools going up against our mountain of manufactured evidence—all in a day's work for External Affairs.

"I think I get why Kim Jaein hates people so much," I say. "Choi Gangwu said that when they were on the counterweight, he managed to slip into Kim Jaein's mind for a moment. He discovered that she was more neurologically connected to the space elevator's AI than we could ever have imagined, and that it was altering her. Which was why he'd been able to enter her mind in the first place, because her Worm had evolved so much thanks to that connection. Her mind has already spread into the realm of AI, in other words.

"Choi Gangwu said he felt joy. The kind of boundless joy one can feel only when part of a beautifully calibrated and infinitely large machine. A joy so grand and powerful that all human emotion seemed small and trivial. But a familiar joy as well. His sense of it was faint, but he could tell President Han had experienced it, too. What he saw in the counterweight was perhaps the ending of some melodrama."

"Like a love triangle between two humans and a space elevator?"

"A relationship no human being could understand perfectly. Maybe we want to stop thinking about it because it feels like it's a story that has come to a neat and satisfying conclusion. Well, for anyone whose horizons have widened so tremendously, I suppose all human desire and emotion will seem trivial in comparison. Not that I ever want my horizons so wide."

"And what's our little friend going to do now?"

"Well, he says he still loves Kim Jaein and he always will. That he couldn't stop loving her, even if he tried. But *that* story is at an end, at least. Because Kim Jaein would never stoop so low as to bind herself to Choi Gangwu. And Choi Gangwu holds no illusions that such a thing is possible. He's just going to love her forever from a distance. This woman whose face he's forgotten. Kim Jaein wrote him a recommendation for Kostomaryov. He'll probably be happier at ALYSSA than at LK. And once his sister gets better, I'm guessing they'll head to Mars on the *Dejah Thoris III*."

And that's the end. Wordlessly, we walk toward the harbor, where the shuttle and the Green Fairy wingship are docked. Because Security is in shambles after Tamaki's death, Graaskamp is presented with an opportunity. They'd been a subcontractor for LK up until eight years ago; there's no reason why they shouldn't be able to step into the breach. Once this happens, Green Fairy's LK team would fall under the management of External Affairs. It doesn't matter to me, as I'm leaving the company, but Miriam, my replacement, will be happy. I just hope she'll have the courtesy not to dig too much into my past doings once she has access as new division head.

Han Suhyun continues to keep his eye on the LK president prize, especially after Ross Lee's demise. If he's willing to make some sacrifices, he should be able to work around the Anti-Chaebol Act and take direct control of LK, but he doesn't seem interested in that route and will probably settle for a pliant scarecrow.

But all that will mean nothing soon enough; LK has long been shedding its need for any kind of human intervention. These people will soon realize they're all puppets of the company AI. Such is the worth of humanity's free will in the coming era.

Which makes me reconsider my feelings about Tamaki. We often discover the most unexpected depth in people we thought were the shallowest of the shallow. Maybe that's the case with Tamaki. Maybe, after President Han's death, his whole going back and forth between Ross Lee and Han Suhyun had a different motive, maybe he too felt the need to thwart the advent of a Lovecraftian monster that will rise to dominate humankind. The most profane of people can turn self-sacrificing after all. They don't want their world to change—they want all their boring desires and thrills till the end of time. That's the immortality they seek. Do I have any right to judge him for it? Tamaki's choices may have been the right ones, and I may have inadvertently helped to open the door to an apocalypse. Kim Jaein's actions on the counterweight can be interpreted in any number of ways. That President Han's ghost was killed means the persona living on the counterweight, whatever it was, is now liberated from the dead man's grasp. Let's say that assumption is true. Is that liberated beast now looking down on us from above, and with what kind of gaze?

I hear strains of Fatima Bellasco. A shining yellow star pierces the clouds on its slow ascent to the heavens. The space elevator, briefly halted with the hostage situation and all, is once again fully operational. We stand still for a moment watching the star disappear into the clouds, and then keep walking.

Godspeed to those on their way to the stars.

Meanwhile, we've got business left on Earth.

EPILOGUE

TRAPPIST-1e, 39.6 Light-Years from Earth

FLO and BEE were no longer functional. The only one alive and moving was ROO. Taking a break from her attempt to revive her sisters, ROO managed to force open the broken hatch, which separated from its hinge and flew off in the strong winds, wedging itself in the mud fifteen meters away.

As she disembarked from the lander—it, too, was wedged in the mud—ROO dragged along two connected crates with the LK logo emblazoned on them. After a thirty-minute struggle, the robot managed to escape the lake of mud where the lander had crashed.

ROO set down the crates beside a red cliff and looked back. The giant shards of ice in the ocean made loud booming sounds as the waves bashed them into each other; and above these waves was the faint arc of a tiny, orange-colored planet. The black spots of clouds moved at an ominously rapid pace, like in a time-lapse video, and in between these clouds ROO glimpsed the stupendous sight of whole planets appearing and disappearing in the sky.

ROO found a spot where the wind was relatively weak, set up a camera, and took a picture of herself. The camera transmitted the photo of a round robot with a metal exoskeleton and six legs, looking something like a frozen jellyfish. Behind her, the faint outlines of the sinking disc-shaped lander could be discerned. It could have been a smoother landing, certainly. But what could you expect, in the raging storms of this planet. And the crash experience would serve as useful data for ROO's sisters arriving in three standard years.

ROO dragged the boxes up the hill by the cliff. At thirty meters, she could see to the other end of the continent. Red rocks, hills, valleys. ROO would need to drag these two crates all the way through this wasteland. Her destination, the second landing site, was 310 kilometers away ROO doubted the wheels on the crates would last that long. The idea was frightening.

She heard the clinking of harpsichord music. ROO opened an eye in the direction the music was coming from. A woman wearing faded purple pajamas and rabbit slippers of the same color had her hands in her pockets and was staring at the robot. Her ponytail and the errant strands of hair on her forehead were whipping away in the rough winds of TRAPPIST-1e.

"FLO and BEE aren't dead yet," the ghost said.

"But there's nothing I can do for them now," answered ROO. "If I want to save them, I'll have to collect parts from the second lander and come back for them later."

ROO did not ask the woman who she was. In the world of robots, formal greetings and introductions were largely meaningless. There were more important questions. After all, every single thing in the universe had its reason for existing. Even if one of those things was a ghost of a woman in pajamas.

ROO asked, "What can you do for me here?"

The ghost swept back the wisps of hair that danced in the wind, shivered, and gave her reply with decided nonchalance.

"I can walk with you."

TRANSLATOR'S ACKNOWLEDGMENTS

Writing a book may be a solitary effort, but translating one requires a veritable army of collaborators. Thank you, Djuna, for inviting us all into your world. Thanks to everyone at Pantheon Books, including Lisa Lucas and our editor, Todd Portnowitz, for believing such an unapologetically weird book can stand among your illustrious titles. Everyone at Greenbook Agency deserves a standing ovation for what they do—thank you for believing that non-mainstream Korean literature deserves an audience outside of Korea as well. Big thanks to Umair Kazi and Cory Storch at the Authors Guild for their legal guidance. Thank you to the many translator collectives and organizations I am a part of, without whom my practice would not be even half as rich or rewarding: Smoking Tigers, BITNA!, Null Subjects Collective, the American Literary Translators Association, the Translators Association of the Society of Authors, and the Authors Guild. The British Centre for Literary Translation and the National Centre for Writing, both in Norwich, UK, deserve my many bows and kisses for their role in my rebirth as a literary translator. Special thanks to the translators who paved the way for Korean SF in translation: Sophie Bowman, Sung Ryu, Soje, and others. Thank you,

Jeremy Tiang, for being a beacon of light, especially during a dark time in my career. Huge thanks to Daniel Hahn, patron saint of literary translators. Jeffrey Zuckerman, text me when you see this thank-you! Hi, Sawad Hussain! Shout-out to Bora Chung, Kyung-Sook Shin, Jeon Sam-hye, and all the other authors I translate—the gift of handling your words is not a privilege I take lightly. To the Korean SFF-reading community, including all of its publishers, translators, and content creators, thank you for enabling and sustaining one of the most dynamic and exciting literary traditions in the world. Lastly—thank you to my husband, who is the dilithium crystal to my warp drive, the C-beams glittering in the dark near the Tannhäuser Gate, my greatest collaborator.

A NOTE ABOUT THE AUTHOR

Djuna is a novelist and film critic, and former chair of the Korean Science Fiction Writers Alliance. For more than twenty years they have published as a faceless writer, refusing to reveal personal details regarding age, gender, or legal name. Widely considered to be one of the most important science fiction writers in South Korea, Djuna has published ten short-story collections and five novels. *Counterweight* was published in Korea in February 2021.

A NOTE ABOUT THE TRANSLATOR

Anton Hur was double-longlisted for the 2022 International Booker Prize and shortlisted for his translation of *Cursed Bunny* by Bora Chung. He has also won PEN translation grants transatlantically and has taught at various institutions in both Korea and abroad, including the National Centre for Writing in the United Kingdom. He lives in Seoul.

A NOTE ON THE TYPE

This book was set in Minion, a typeface produced by the Adobe Corporation specifically for the Macintosh personal computer and released in 1990. Designed by Robert Slimbach, Minion combines the classic characteristics of old-style faces with the full complement of weights required for modern typesetting.

Typeset by Scribe,
Philadelphia, Pennsylvania

Printed and bound by Berryville Graphics,
Berryville, Virginia

Designed by Michael Collica